MOONS OF TRIOPUS

By the same author

ONE IS ONE
NEVER THE SAME DOOR
INTERSTELLAR TWO-FIVE

MOONS OF TRIOPUS

by

JOHN RANKINE

London
DENNIS DOBSON

First published in Great Britain in 1968 by
Dobson Books Ltd, 80 Kensington Church Street, London W.8.

Printed in Great Britain by

WILLMER BROTHERS LIMITED,
BIRKENHEAD.

SBN 234 77196 8

Chapter One

One step ends a multi-billion kilometre journey. Taken in squalor, its backward-working gloss colours what has gone before.

Not that the low-level mono-rail from Western Metropolitan Space Port was uniformly squalid. Commander Grant D. Kirby was seeing it with a disenchanted eye.

It ran below angled, striding legs of continuous building blocks. Daylight fell coldly on a chequer board of pink and grey paving thirty metres below its hurrying shuttles. Litter swirled in spirals and sank as the cars passed. Foreshortened figures of unscheduled-class vagrants moved on aimless missions over its concrete deserts. Filling in time between subsistence handouts.

After twelve month's absence it was an aspect of Earth which was hard to reconcile. Even knowing that they were worthless to themselves and the towering stratified society above them made it no easier to take.

Light had something to do with his mood. After the clear Umbrian day of Triopus, this mixture of harsh, natural daylight and glare from spaced-out ceiling ports was clinical and depressing.

Kirby felt that ever since *Europa Nine* had blazed down to its designated pad, he had been in a long tube. Nor was that only physical fact. His mind was blinkered, so that he could only see one way and what he saw he liked less and less.

Six seats in the VIP compartment. Four faces that he knew too well. Even in counterpoint time, the mission to Triopus had taken over a hundred days each way. Together with three months on the green planet it was more than enough to bring personalities into head-on confrontation.

Facing him, Dr Boris Martinez, high-shouldered and urbane, was leaning back, stroking four long sinewy fingers across his spreading forehead in a habitual gesture which now grated on Kirby's nerves.

He had seen it too often as a prelude to some compromise which pleased no-one. As titular head of the expedition, Martinez had been too much inclined to bow to pressure groups inside. Probably not corrupt; but making it very easy for the commercial interests to push dangerous policy.

Next to him, Mark Hadden sat erect. Sideburns, black moustache, very neat. Large brown eyes meeting Kirby's with a query which was plain enough, 'What are you going to do about it, then?' Another element too, which could be simple malice or prior knowledge of something Kirby did not know, but which was definitely against his interest.

Kirby recognized that he had never liked Hadden. Competent enough as a civil engineering specialist, but basically a creep. Dangerous in this instance. His manipulation of Martinez had been very successful.

On his own side of the car, Glen Watkins and Sally Maloon talking together in low confidential tones. Not quite in secrecy, but definitely a personal, one-to-one net. Classic yes-men. Not an original idea between them. Solidly behind Martinez right or wrong. The Maloon, as the doctor's personal assistant, perhaps owed him that much loyalty, but Watkins as the expedition's resident head-shrinker ought to know better.

That left Gary Ward, physicist, an unlikely ally for a military man; but the only member of the hierarchy to see it his way.

Between them though, they should be able to swing it. Ward was well known and his opinions had to be heard. Their minority report could not be suppressed and was sure to get enough support to put in a veto on plans for any large-scale population moves to Triopus.

Kirby checked his time disk. Only three or four minutes at most before they reached the Department for Extra Terrestrial Colonization. There would be a reception lined up no doubt. Triopus was big news. Eventually though, the crunch would come and Ward's unwelcome words would be spoken.

Where was Ward anyway? Better keep together. Ward was a fighter and would not need any stiffening, but every man liked some support. They must sit near together at the conference.

He ran over their agreed strategy in his mind. No improvement suggested itself. They would leave it until they were asked formally if they supported the account given by Martinez. Cued in by the Establishment its own self, Ward's dissent would have a greater impact. Then there was the document they had spent long hours on. Ward had it ready to hand over, together with some recorded interviews with Triopus notables to show that its people had a culture and could not be ignored.

After that Kirby himself as second-in-command of the expedition could come in with support.

He knew that it would be fatal if the minority report appeared to be mainly his devising. Alone in the higher echelon, he was not an academic. He was in as a military director, on secondment from Western Hemisphere Space Command to run the practical side of the expedition for its civilian committee.

From the beginning, he had been made to feel that Martinez and his staff could have managed fine without him. Never pushed to an open breach; but there all right. They resented the directive which had forced the Extra Terrestrial Department to include a military director on the management committee.

Well, it was all over. They would be even less pleased when he and Ward had said their piece. He would be well out of it. Get back to his own ship and a new mission without civilian complications. Where was Ward then?

Kirby stood up and sidestepped into the central aisle of the speeding shuttle. Conscious that Hadden's eyes followed him, he went down the short passageway to the observation deck in its bullet nose. Misnamed that when you got down to it,

7

there was damn all to observe, except the dirty white underbelly of the social heap and endless hectares of slab floor.

Ward was not there.

Nudged by a sixth sense signalling danger, Kirby swung on his heel and went back.

This car had been put at the sole disposal of *Europa Nine*'s executive. Not even an official had come along to monitor its robot gear. Thirty paces took him to the rear platform, identical to the leading end and equally empty.

He watched himself walking into it. Very tall and elongated further by the curved reflecting surface of its panoramic windshield. Olive green uniform tunic with a round stiff collar. Long face, accentuated now in an El Greco distortion. Close-cropped brown hair, hallmark of the veteran space man, ageing him much beyond his thirty-seven years. Eyes penetrating and grey-flecked, fairly snapping now as suspicion hardened to certainty that something was rotten in the state.

He went back checking each alcove, trying to remember when exactly he had last seen Ward.

There had been three halts. Short waits in loop lines to give way for regular city services, which ran to a tight schedule and could not be hung up without passing back a ripple of dislocation. Last one of these, five minutes back, had lasted a full minute. Now he saw in flashback that Ward had moved at that time, bound for the washroom.

So what? Nobody could have expected that and based a play on it.

Kirby levelled with the occupied zone again. Hadden called out, 'What is it, Commander, you look worried?'

Trust that creep to use a title. Kirby said flatly, 'I'm looking for Ward.'

'Well, unless he's taken wing, he shouldn't be far to seek.'

Sensitive now to every harmonic, Kirby felt the underlying sneer. As though Hadden had prior knowledge that Ward would be hard to find.

8

He made no reply and went over his first route to the forward deck checking two remaining alcoves. Then he slid back the washroom hatch.

Like a drum in a videophone kiosk, Ward was not to be missed.

He was propped with his forehead against the outer bulkhead, legs braced out in a nicely calculated V to give tripod support. As the shuttle smoothly decelerated, to bring them in to the terminal, his garnered kinetic urge pivoted him on his left foot in a zombie pirouette and turned him to face the seeker.

Meticulously centred on his forehead, a centimetre below the hair line, a small, red, bodkin hole was full and satisfactory explanation of his absence.

Whatever was essentially personal of Dr G. Ward had taken flight for a sure thing.

With a slight, pneumatic recoil, the shuttle centred itself to a millimetre at the marks set for its reception. Entry ports sliced back. Without actually rolling one out, there was an aura of red carpet on the white-tiled platform. Kirby, steadying the cadaver with one hand and looking out, saw a knot of welcoming officials. At least one uniform with the blue tabs of high-ranking staff, a tall girl with fair hair severely taken back, newsmen with a camera crew to take proceedings live.

He knew without looking for it, how it would be. Ward's report would be gone. His own unaided testimony would be discounted. Moved at a deeper level than conscious thought, he went into action. Gathering up Ward in a fireman's lift, he backed out of the cubby hole and was still first out into the blaze of light.

Focussing on the military representative, identified now as General Wilkes, head of the military escort wing, he went straight forward and tipped his biological trash on the parquet like an intelligent bird dog.

Conventional welcome died the death. Martinez and the rest, crowding up behind, went largely ignored. Kirby said harshly, 'I have no pleasure at all in presenting this minority report. I'd like it filed wherever is convenient.'

It took all of three hours for Kirby to recognize that his excellent opening gambit was not going to change a thing.

When the confusion stabilized itself and the machinery of welcome slipped back into gear, he was no further forward. In fact, his curt announcement was being wilfully misunderstood and Ward's murder was treated as a political assassination, engineered by a bogy underground which the establishment brought out for an airing whenever it had a controversial matter under review. Fear of an unknown enemy of the state could be relied on to stifle the liberals in the administration and sent the more definite opposition into discreet silence. No one wanted to be put on the unscheduled list and spend the rest of a lifetime in the concrete wastes.

Quick thinking on the part of a sweet-scented PRO had tripped the outgoing sound beam before he made his speech. The public at large had only seen the tall commander carry out a body and tip it callously on the deck. Even though it wasn't a dog it did his image no good.

Reception, with a banquet and a dozen toasts, had gone on. Now they were waiting in an oval conference room for the Minister of Colonization himself.

Kirby had been nobody's friend.

Martinez had resented his action as detracting from the achievements of the expedition and as disloyalty to himself. The Senator for colonial affairs had seen it as a bid for publicity and a pitch for unilateral decision without the due process of debate.

General Wilkes had seen it as a setback for the military image already tarnished and hung about by too many civilian restrictions as it was. This would strengthen the hand of those members of the governmental committees who distrusted the military arm and had the power to restrict its funds.

The oval conference room was on the two-hundred and-fifty-third floor of the ETC complex. Its long observation ports were set high and served by a continuous gallery lined now by observers and publicity men. From the well, with its rows of executive desks, there was only grey blue sky to see. As though they were in the suspended gondola of an airbag traffic post.

Triopus with its unique impact of sun and air on the skin seemed incredibly remote. Kirby had to force himself time and time again to believe that the smooth flow of polispeak had any meaning at all.

Facts and figures were in any case on an unimaginable scale. In their absence, preparations had gone forward. Triopus or not, colonization would go on somewhere. For one thing it was big business. Transports, building at satellite stations to ferry a first draft of a hundred thousand people, had filled order books for every space engineering outfit in the hemisphere. Also there was latter-day nationalist pride to get in first before the Eastern scheme got off the ground.

Martinez presented his case well. Much photogenic smoothing of his wide forehead. Voice suave and persuasive, using an intercom which he scarcely needed to be heard round the quiet room.

Sally Maloon keyed in some official interviews with selected leaders of Triopus communities. Soft spoken gentle voices, bird-like and delicate in this setting, presented in instant translation at every desk.

They did not oppose contact with the strangers. Triopus had huge empty lands. New settlements would not worry them as long as their own way of life was not disturbed.

That was a laugh. How long would they continue undisturbed once the city-builders got under way? Specimens on a reservation. Tolerated until their land was needed and then conform or go under. They were ready-made to wander as unscheduled classes on the concrete desert that would lie below the new cities.

11

Except that Kirby believed they were not typical. The lost records made by Wade showed the reverse of the coin. Some had come out definitely against the idea and hinted that there was power at their disposal to give them a choice.

The weakness of his case was that he did not know what they meant. Only a memory that it had been utterly convincing to himself and Ward.

Sally Maloon had put out a videotape and he saw again the long lawn-like vistas surrounding the township near *Europa Nine*. A small settlement with wide avenues, delicate tamarisk fronds against low houses. Pink and white adobe, single storey; flat roofs; a network of blue canals with square-nosed barges bringing in produce from the farms. No movement quicker than walking pace. What possible power could they have? It seemed as ridiculous to him now as it could possibly do to the committed faction.

Camera shots took them right in to the central square and face to face with people. Small, slender, dark-skinned. A young woman, hair elaborately piled in a spiral of thin electrum, slim to the point of emaciation. Wearing a short red kaftan and high-heeled sandals, walking with short steps so that she seemed to glide.

Seeing it again reminded him that there were few of the very old or very young in the streets. A curious sense of a timeless society.

Time was getting on. There would be little opportunity for discussion this session. No doubt they would be in and out of the conference room for a week before the final decisions were taken. But a news-hungry public would be delighted with this first-report. Any lingering impact of Ward's death was long gone.

He was surprised to hear his own name. Senator Costall, who never knowingly missed a cliché, was asking him directly as second-in-command if he had anything to add to the brief.

Kirby pushed the angle-poise mike out of the way and spoke

straight across the floor to the facing line of government reps. Costall himself in the centre lifted his head from a littered desk and seemed ready to listen. He was a heavily-built man with shoulders like an ox and a grey face. Emotion would have to work like a beaver to bring animation to his boiled blue eyes. Aesthetics were a dead duck. Only facts would get to first base.

Kirby said, 'Everything which has been reported is true enough. But it is not the whole story. Acceptance of the project is not universal. The late Dr Ward had a line on it. His notes and the report we worked on together have gone. Now you have only my unsupported word. I am convinced that much closer investigation should be made before a colonizing fleet goes out.'

Martinez was working overtime on his forehead-stroking ploy. Hadden leaned over to him and said something inaudible, but clearly on the not-to-worry tack.

Every eye was on Kirby and he had time to see that he was a minority of one. Behind the front bench, a clutter of advisers looked impatient. Months of detailed preparatory work was in the balance. They were committed to a man to press for progress.

Alone amongst them, a severe and symmetrical blonde head remained bent over a desk littered with data. One at least dismissed the interruption as an irrelevance soon to be ironed out.

Kirby said, 'It is not in my interest to oppose this plan. I have no concessions to gain or any political angle. I know the research that has been needed to find Triopus and I agree that it appears to be an ideal setting for a new colony. But the Galactic Organization's Charter is clear enough. There must be agreement with local life forms if they come within the definitions laid down. You have seen the people. You can be in no doubt about their culture level.'

Senator Costall's gravel voice came across the quiet room.

13

He too ignored his intercom. 'Are they aware of their rights under the charter?'

'Yes.'

'You made sure of that.'

It was a flat statement rather than a question and nettled Kirby with its suggestion that he was some kind of fifth column.

'That question would be asked anyway by any Galactic Commissar giving agreement to the project. It is surely not suggested that we disregard the Galactic Organization in this?'

'That is a political matter, Commander, where your opinion is not canvassed.'

'I have worked on liaison with the Galactic Organization. They will insist that their requirements are met. From my own experience, I would say that they are more likely to think that a link with our own Eastern Hemisphere Colonial Office would be more desirable for Triopus. The ethnic gap would be less obvious. As you saw, they are a dark-skinned people. Not unlike the ancient races of Cambodia. But that, I will agree is another issue and not my affair.'

Costall swivelled in his seat for a word with one of the specialists behind him and Kirby waited for his attention.

When he went on, his voice was level and matter-of-fact. It was a hunch he was defending. Nothing that could be classified and punched out for a computer. 'I believe that the people of Triopus have means to resist a large-scale landing if they become convinced that it is against their interest. What you have seen shows them to be harmless and peaceful. So they are. But it is an ancient culture. They have discarded a great deal of technical know-how which we still find important. That is not to say they have forgotten it. I was personally convinced that it was no idle threat when my contacts said they could and would make effective resistance.'

'Such as what?'

'I do not know.'

Exhaled sighs of impatience and relief from many. Costall

himself waited a full minute before he delivered judgment.

'You must agree, Commander, that you have had a fair hearing. I believe you are sincere and I accept that you have no personal axe to grind. But you are asking too much. The Triopus project is no new thing. As you appreciate, the chance of finding such a suitable site is very small. What you have said will be recorded.'

He looked at the time disk on his console. 'I must also record the thanks of the administration for the loyal work of the first expedition to Triopus. Dr Martinez and his team have done well in the short time they had there. The reports will have detailed study and another conference will be called for this day week. You will all be glad I am sure to pick up the threads again on Earth planet.'

Back in his rooms in the reception area for distinguished guests of the establishment, Grant Kirby flicked on a wall-to-wall actualizer and got himself up-to-date on current affairs.

It was, anyway, simpler than thought. He had come to the conclusion that he would ask to be returned to normal duties. If the Galactic Organization gave their okay, there was nothing he could do about it. Who was he to stand in as public conscience on Triopus? Non-technical civilizations had gone under before and would again. The logic of time and sophistication was against them.

His room was peopled with 3-D shadows and flooded with a sexy scent. A girl from an alpha level had gotten herself emotionally involved with a gamma-plus, food-staple processor. Eugenics had put in a veto on their pairing application and they were hiding out in a sleazy run-down tenement only just above ground level.

Now she was having second thoughts and it was a sure thing that the social proprieties were going to be vindicated. Any script man working any other conclusion could kiss good-bye to his contract.

Kirby tuned out the sound. Watching them mime it out made the dilemma even more false. Like every other impasse, its weakness lay in the premise.

Accustomed to looking at the blue planet from outside, he saw the differences between people, high level-low level, West-East, old-young, male-female as so small that any big issue raised on them as a platform was ridiculous from the start. For him there were only people.

The big difference came when you compared planetary cultures. Now if that Epstein-eyed girl had been entrained with an eggheaded insect man from Chrysaor there would have been a case for the prosecution.

He had reached this point in internal debate, when a new feature came up. They had got on to it quickly at that. The wall filled with a free-standing banner headline, 'COULD THIS BE YOUR NEW HOME?' Underneath in smaller type, 'The Green and Lovely World of Triopus. Applications for Emigration Now Considered. There is still a place for you.'

Kirby turned up the sound and got an ad-man's patter over an edited version of Sally Maloon's pictures.

On the return trip, he had dropped into a familiar world of space-navigation and had not been too nostalgic about what he had left. This second showing, with the actualizer bringing people life-size into his private room, brought it all back. That and the contrast. These delicate and dignified figures against the half-baked mush of the preceding play.

Kirby resented the responsibility which was settling on him. He and Ward had done their best. Probably, when you got right down to it there was nothing conclusive the Triopusians could do. Earth's advanced and teeming billions could not be stopped by a handful of aesthetes. Not even if they could resurrect some power which seemed sufficient to them. They could not know what they were up against.

Well, he had a few weeks leave. Stay with it. Put in a word

where he could. Try Wilkes privately. He would know that there was no hidden motive in it.

It was a decision of a kind and Kirby was satisfied to make it. He liked a blue print for action.

He stood watching the scene for another minute and then switched out.

Ten seconds later he was making his erect and long-legged way along a wide circulation corridor.

Kirby had an elevator to himself. He dropped down a hundred levels for the main thoroughfares of the city. It was nineteeen hundred hours and the walkways were filling up with crowds moving from their apartments to the gastronomic centres.

Four minutes in the fast lane and he was out through reduction bays to a square which ran up to a ceiling fifty levels above and a blue-black night sky simulator with a moving planetarium of stars.

The perimeter was a welter of tube lighting. Theatres, eating houses. A dancing nude worked in blue asterisks. It was pleasant enough to lose identity in a crowd after the long months in an enclave.

Kirby took his time, walking slowly round the piazza. When he found himself back at his starting point, it was nineteen thirty-five and he reckoned it was all of two kilometres for the round trip.

A second factor, which his computer punched out for attention, was that while the crowd changed continuously, some of its elements in his own orbit had remained constant.

There was a small man in the blue overalls of a gamma-class operative and a thick-set man in lower-admin grey who had almost certainly been with him over on the far side beneath the indefatigable nude.

Kirby began a second circuit, stopping every now and then and checking back. Two-thirds round and there wasn't a doubt left.

17

He went under the garish canopy of a sea-food delicatessen and through a fronded sea-weed curtain to its bizarre dining-room.

The computers at the 'Portuguese Man of War' claimed to have worked the ultimate on piscine simulates from the basic staples. Table directories listed two hundred and six choices on direct dialling and a promise that anything not recorded would be made for a choosy patron with time to spare and a ten-per-cent surcharge.

It was almost full and Kirby edged into a red plush bench seat with his back to a long wall mirror. On his right a family party was eating through a small mountain of salmon kedgeree with sombre determination and close left an opulent red head was telling her attentive friend about something that had scandalized her at the office.

Assassination here would be tricky to work in safety, if that was the aim. He dialled for Paupiettes de Sole a La Richelieu which was coded elaborately and allowed him to fiddle with a broad knife and angle it to reflect from the mirror over his shoulder. He saw them come in separately and sit one by the door and one at the far side under a blue arrow which pointed the seeker to the men's room.

There was a pattern in that. Like Ward. With a swift laser shot to make his quietus. Kirby felt a tingling in his nerves. For him, in the past, danger had come impersonally. Strapped in an acceleration couch on the command island of a hurrying ship. An intellectual exercise. Something to be worked at with mathematics and the fast handling of computer-fed data.

This time it was a personal issue and he wondered briefly how he would make out.

But when his meal was eaten and he had keyed in his identity references for credit restrictions, he stood up casually and made for the street exit. Halfway there, he changed direction as though on impulse and oriented himself by the blue arrow.

There was an ante room with magazines and beyond it an inner sanctum with flattering provision for Everyman.

He waited just inside the second door flat against a bulkhead, and heard the slight hiss of the first hatch slicing back. The quick step of a small man in a hurry and the blue coveralls came through and past him.

Kirby spoke quietly from behind. 'Looking for me?'

Doubt evaporated as the man came round like a snake. His reflexes were fast, but Kirby was used to the split-second re-actions of space navigation. He had a neck lock on which made his question pure rhetoric. No answer could have been made even if there had been a good one.

A silvery oblong box, near enough to a cigarette case to be unremarkable, clattered to the parquet. Kirby increased pressure and the man stopped trying. But suffering seldom purifies. As soon as the grip eased, he brought his knee up in an old-fashioned ploy which deserved no better than it got.

Kirby took it on his right hip and grabbed the moving leg sure and true. When the man's head hit the floor he lay still with his eyes setting in a pale and terminal glare. Any questions about who had set him on his mission would need a crystal ball.

The hiss of the far door made a period. Kirby gathered in the box and had checked out its mechanism when the thick set man joined them.

As the door sliced back, the newcomer saw enough to recognize that he should report to base. He was crossing the anteroom and moving well when Kirby shot him meticulously through the back of his head. He did not hear 'That's for Ward.' Nor did he know about it when he and his colleague were propped convincingly in adjoining cubicles as long-sitting tenants.

Kirby salved his conscience by checking out a second laser and went thoughtfully into the square.

Employers of such agents were not likely to want to make a big thing about it. He was safe enough from civil proceedings.

But if two, there could be more. He would have to be very careful indeed.

Eastbound walkways were thinning out and that was bad. Half way home, he took reduction bays to a small residential square and went up fifty levels. Then he walked along a circulation corridor towards the Colonization Block.

He still had a kilometre to go and he tried to think it out.

Alone, he was a sitting target. Whoever wanted him out of it could find ways and means. He had to sleep. He needed allies.

At an intersection, he saw a videophone kiosk and went inside. No-one in sight could be an agent. A few women bringing children back from their evening meal for bed. An elderly man in sneakers and faded blue coveralls doing a repair job on his apartment door.

Kirby looked for Wilkes, General Howard B.

When the man came up, head and shoulders on the screen, he was obviously less than delighted to see Kirby. But he stuck to an ambivalent form of words. 'What can I do for you, Commander?'

'I'd like a few minutes of your time, General.'

'Now?'

'My time could be limited. I've just missed finishing up in the same club as Ward.'

'Where are you now?'

Kirby checked the kiosk identification tag. 'Box J/7082 Intersection 63/94 on Fifty.'

'Stay where you are, I'll send an escort.'

'That won't be necessary, General. Where can I see you?'

The answer came with just that shade of hesitation which made Kirby wonder where the escort would have taken him. Wilkes must be clean. Just not anxious to tarnish his image.

'Very well, Commander. I'll expect you here in about fifteen minutes. 235 level in the Ministry Block. Well signposted. There's a party on, but they'll pass you through to my suite.'

When Kirby got inside the door he felt as out of place as a nun at a coven. Walking behind a dapper major-domo in a black dress uniform of the ground service corps, he threaded his way through a crowded hexagonal hall. Top level civilians, full of phatic chat, looked him up and down as though he had made an inopportune call to service a disposal unit. Through open double doors, stage left, another shifting pattern of white and gold and electrum. Women in every style current in the galaxy. Waiters weaving about.

They reached centre and his guide through the underworld paused to give a deferential tap on the facing door. Kirby looked back and a fortuitous opening of the crowd left him looking at a tall blonde girl he had surely seen before somewhere.

Hair severely taken back. Wearing a high-necked cheongsam in black silk. Face mathematically exact on a broad oval. Unsmiling in a serious considering look until the ranks closed and she was instantly lost.

Chapter Two

Kirby said, 'General. Whatever the merits, somebody wants a hundred per cent certainty that nothing slows up the project for Triopus. Nothing can be sure at that level.'

In civilian rig, Wilkes could have been a retired business exec. Kirby saw, for the first time, that the man was ageing. Probably knocking on for a last year of office. Even before the General spoke, he knew that he had not found a friend.

They were in a large, elegant room with an elaborate actualizer set with its own stage, proscenium arch complete. That and the expensive shindig outside was on a credit scale beyond the range of most service personnel even in the highest echelons. The general was doing all right and wanted it to stay that way.

He said reasonably, 'Look, Commander, let's say that you are less than satisfied with the project for Triopus. I believe you have doubts which seem sufficient to you. Ward's death, and the attack now on yourself, confirm you in thinking that nobody wants to know. All right. Don't think for a minute that I don't see the serious angles. But try to see it from this side of the fence.'

Kirby, stretched out against his will in a feather-soft lounge chair, holding a brandy glass worth a month's credits, felt that Wilkes had not sat at Costall's feet in vain.

The General went on, 'Mounting this operation has been a fantastic effort. Stopping it, or even slowing it behind schedules would bring economic chaos. Then there are the human angles. A hundred thousand in the first stage. With family contacts, it's a million involved people. Public confidence comes into it. All you can oppose, is a hunch. It should be no surprise to you that you are not liked.'

'I should think the department was big enough to take opposition without getting out the long knives.'

'The department isn't involved in that. You know the way society has gone here. Perhaps you don't though. Service personnel can get pretty isolated on constant missions and in their own enclave. It's easy to pick up a couple of killers. Do you know how many unsolved deaths the security branch in this city had on their files for the last civic year?'

Kirby sat up. He was being handed a smooth line which seemed to be taking his own personal problem out of context.

Wilkes said, 'There were sixteen hundred odd for this city alone. That's more than four a day. You can pick up a killer for the price of a drink. Business men can sabotage a rival firm anytime they like. Among the thousand of firms working on the project, there must be dozens who couldn't afford it to stop and possibly some who would take extreme steps to see that no criticism was voiced. You don't have to look to the politicians for enemies.'

'How would anybody know what Ward was going to say?'

'That I don't know. It looks like a leak. Remember *Europa Nine* was signalling news flashes for the last month before you came in.'

'I see all that. What do you suggest from now on?'

'Return to your unit. I'll talk to your Squadron Controller. He'll put you back on your ship. No criticism on a military level has been made. In fact Martinez has put in an extremely good report on your work for the expedition. Does that surprise you?'

'No. I have no direct quarrel with Martinez. I think he was badly advised and too ready to look at the credit side.'

'You can stay here, if you like, tonight. It might be safer for you. Join your unit in the morning.'

Wilkes was looking more pleased. As though he had rounded a difficult corner. Kirby was suddenly sickened by the whole business. Okay, let them have it. This kind of intrigue was no

23

good. Forget it. Get back to his ship where there was a straight-forward job to do. But until then, he could look after himself. Or not as the case might be. Either way it hardly mattered.

He stood up and put his glass symmetrically on a table. 'That's all right, General. I get the message loud and clear. Perhaps you've hit the truth of it. It's nothing to do with me. If you can get a signal to Squadron Controller Halsall, I'd be glad. I'll make my way to Preston sometime tomorrow.'

A melodramatic pinger drew attention to a miniature video-phone on an ornate desk in an alcove. From the distance, the fist-sized face of the caller was hardly identifiable. An impression that the head was large in proportion to the shoulders below it and that it was exceptionally pale and bald.

Wilkes made no attempt to answer and Kirby moved to the door. 'I'll see myself out. Goodnight.'

He was through into the busy anteroom, before Wilkes could ring for a guide.

Two more bleeps from the video and Wilkes moved over to it. He said, 'What can I do for you at this hour, Chairman?'

The voice that sprang breathily from the desk top was soft and sibilant. Oskar Lasmec, head of a consortium with twenty-nine billion credits tied up in the Triopus project was used to getting attention without verbal emphasis. He was also one for the direct approach.

'Commander Kirby has been to visit you, General.'

'Yes. He wanted advice.'

'I'm sure he received good council.'

'He has given up any thought of opposing the project. He is returning to his unit tomorrow.'

'Then he did have good advice.'

'Thank you.'

'Not at all, General, not at all. You will find we are grateful. As indeed you have found in the past, eh General?'

'It was genuine enough on his part. He really believes there could be trouble.'

'And what is a little trouble? That's life, General, isn't it? And if the people of Triopus make trouble they will have to be settled once and for all. In some ways it might be better if they do. Once permission is granted, the Galactic Commission will accept a certain use of force to make a settlement safe.'

'How is that going?'

'I am glad to say, no further delay is expected. The clearance document will be through in the next few days. Has your Commander talked to anyone else?

'He is not my Commander. No, I believe not.'

'Good. Good. Well perhaps you would be good enough to see that he stays safely at his post and concentrates on his military duties. It might be better if he had a spell with some base installation. Unless he does that, I would not give a great deal for his chances of survival. Too many people would feel insecure. You understand me, General?'

'I understand you very well.'

'Then I will say goodnight.'

'Goodnight, Chairman.'

As the screen blanked, Kirby reached the outer door. If anything, there were more people about. He saw the back of a fair head with a wrist-thick rope of pale hair, lustrous in gold filigree bands, going down out of sight in the press. He found himself speculating how long it was and an obscure associative link dredged up the nursery tale of Rapunzel. Hair like that gave it credibility. A cable to climb by. Then he was at the door and letting himself out.

Grant Kirby slept like a cat. Executive officers on *Cossack* had reason to doubt whether he slept at all. Whatever the hour, he would answer a call on his cabin intercom as though he had been there all the time with his finger on the switch.

It was a faculty in part natural and in part cultivated and it had saved minutes when seconds were important. When the heating duct grid in his sitting room was pushed out and lowered with patient care to the thick-piled floor cover, he sat up in bed and looked automatically at his time disk.

It was 0500 hours. Venetian blinds run back, gave a panoramic view of black sky with a grey bar of dawnlight bottom left. When he was standing just inside his bedroom door he could pick up a slight scruff of movement somewhere above head height in the outer room. Simultaneously, there was a subdued hiss from the door on to the corridor. Someone had overridden the inner lock mechanism and the motor was doing its best to slice the partition back.

Plastic wedges, won from behind floor-to-ceiling furniture units, were enough to take care of that, so he concentrated on the aerial ballet.

To his own surprise, Kirby found that an uncontrollable muscular tick had started up in the muscles of his left arm. He had experienced fear before. Fear that by some failure of skill his ship would not survive the next half minute. Fear that in the event he would suddenly be unable to act.

Now it was a new thing. It was deeply personal. Here he was involved alone. Hunted and trapped. He knew that he did not want to die.

A thought came that it was better to be living as an unscheduled-class nomad, than be a dead hero. Then anger swamped it out. He forced his left arm to reach out and stub down the light switch and with the action, he ceased to think about himself at all.

When the light flared out he had his eyes closed and was less dazzled than the man in black coveralls and sneakers who was dropping at full arm stretch from an open, metre-square air duct.

Still in the duct, head and shoulders into the room a second was staring at him with wide open eyes and trying to bring his right hand from where it was still jammed by his side.

Kirby took him first using his heavy service laser and an angry red slit from a falling shot bisected the man's forehead.

He stopped trying and then began to move back.

There was time to register that some other agency than his own must be working from behind, before the groundling was round and coming across the carpet.

He had only an Iron Age bowie knife. It would have been made to look like a thuggee robbery-with-violence job. It was flicking out for Kirby's chest when the laser hissed briefly again and the man's dying momentum brought him on into the doorway.

Kirby sidestepped and let him fall. Up above there was an empty hole. Whoever was behind would have to drag back to a junction before he could pass. If he wanted to pass. Only a suicide would come on again.

Standing on a table Kirby reached for the sill and drew himself up to look over it, with the hair on his scalp prickling. He was in time to see a limp hand scrabble out of sight like a pale rat. Ten metres down, the conduit turned sharply left.

One thing was for sure, he was tired of being on the receiving end. He went to the door, listened, then drew out his wedges. Pressing the button he stood clear, ready to fire; but the opening was blank and when he looked out, the corridor was empty.

Back in his bedroom, he fished out slacks and a check shirt, buckled on his service belt and shoved his laser into its clip. He heaved the late prowler on to his bed and covered him like a regular sleeper. Then he piled a chair on a table, put out the light, and took an easy way into the conduit.

Now that there was no light behind him, he could see a faint glow ahead. There was no sound of movement and he made his own, slow—very deliberate, with long pauses to listen.

After the bend, there was a run of five metres and a blank wall ahead, lit marginally from the right. Drag marks identified the right hand turn as the way to go. This was a main shaft with room to crawl. He counted three more openings on his right leading out to other suites, before the human mat showed him the way.

Another sixty-degree angle, light strengthening all the way, and he was facing a lighted grille.

There was no doubt they were still in the VIP wing of the Colonization Block. It would be interesting to know who played host to the cutting-out party.

Moving a centimetre at a time, he got up close and was looking down on a room similar to his own. As far as he could tell, it was empty and there was no sound of voice or movement.

It was hot in the duct and he was streaked with sweat and dust. He got his hands out in front and put his laser ready beside the grille, then he began to push, remembering too late that the grille in his own room had been lowered on cords.

It came clear with a jerk and he took its weight in one hand, whipping up his laser with the other. But when his head was through he could see that the room was empty indeed except for the studio portrait of a bald man in a gilt frame angled to face him on a small occasional table.

Five seconds later, he was out and standing clear. Aware now that the place had a definite feminine aura with delicate overtones of sandalwood.

He was still checking it out, when the bedroom door opened and the only begetter of this *luxe calme et volupté* appeared before his very eyes in a translucent flame shift.

It was Rapunzel in the flesh and there was no mystery about how far the rope of blonde hair would reach. It was over her left shoulder in a thick ringlet and hung precisely to her hip. Adding an interesting line to the classical equilateral triangle formed by shadowy breasts and a darkly recessive navel.

Aesthetics however were at a discount. He said harshly, 'Hold it there. Stand still.'

It was an unnecessary injunction. She was already standing very still with an unconscious *déhanchement* which would have had Ingres grabbing for a lump of charcoal.

She said reasonably, 'Who are you and what are you doing here?'

It was a good speech for the time of day and he reluctantly admired the patrician tone of it. Unfairly, he countered with a question of his own, 'Where are the men who were in here just now?'

In spite of the harshness, she recognized that he was not primarily concerned about herself. It was no personal threat, but urgent enough. She had always wanted to use the line, so she said, 'They went thataway,' and pointed to the outer door.

'How do you know that?'

'I don't, but they certainly didn't come into my room. I'd notice a thing like that.'

Some of the tension eased out of him. After the events of the last twenty-four hours it was relief of a kind to meet even this wry civility.

'Back inside. I'll check.'

She stood her ground until he was two paces off and then turned away in a move that could have been haughty in full dress.

Certainly the room was empty except for a bed and fixed furniture which could only hold a midget.

'What's through there?'

'A bathroom.'

He went in and again it was true. Fluttering from the warm air vent, a pair of flimsy briefs were the sole moving occupants.

It was a small intimate sidelight on her household management, which made her suddenly very human. The last of anger drained away.

When he came out, she had zipped herself into a long green housecoat. He put the laser into its clip and said, 'I had to be sure. You've had other visitors, whether you know it or not. Used your ventilator grille to get through to my room. That's the second time they've tried to have me join Ward. It's a pity the committee can't seen any farther than their own damned noses.'

'I didn't know it. But now I recognize you. Commander Kirby, isn't it?'

'Yes.'

'As one of the "damned committee" I might say that you can't expect anything else. Do you appreciate what this project means?'

'I'm beginning to. I've had that line from Wilkes. Don't give it me all again. You haven't met the people of Triopus. I have. You're all blinkered by facts and figures. What's so marvellous about Western culture that you want to spawn it all over the galaxy? I tell you there's something to be lost on Triopus which can't be made over. Quite apart from another thing, which is equally a fact, that it won't be as easy as you all want to make out.'

She was looking at him as though for the first time. At the conference, she had written him off as a military type with a private vendetta against civilian planning. They were common enough and she had met opposition on other Colonization ploys to make her detest the breed. Now she knew at least that this one was sincere.

'You really believe that.' It was said as a statement.

'I believe it. But now you can get on with it. I'll go back to my unit and that can't be too soon for me.'

'You won't attend the next meeting?'

'I have nothing to add to what I said.'

She went off on another tack and although he could not say that he had made a convert, she was no longer in open dislike. 'You had better wash yourself before you go outside. A security patrol could pick you up as a vagrant.'

'Security? That's a laugh for a start. But thank you. I'll do that.'

At the door she said, 'Don't worry too much about it, Commander. The force that's going out is too big to be in any danger. I'm on the logistics staff. I can tell you it's immense. And your Triopus people won't come to any harm. We observe the Galactic Human Rights Charter. Not everyone in the project is dishonest.'

He could have said that his own rights to stay on the quick side of the human equation had been lately in eclipse; but it was too early in the morning for argument. He said, 'I hope you are right.'

It was not until he was outside his own door that he realized he still didn't know her name.

Squadron Controller Halsall, a big man, with radiation burns across his forehead and a neat piece of cybernetic engineering as stand-in for his left arm, was more irritable than usual. 'Look, Grant, you've stirred up a hell of a stink out there. I've had the devil's own job to keep you in your command slot. Give me the facts and straight. You're damned lucky. I can see through that old tart Wilkes. Anything he says I know must be twisted all to hell. What's it about?'

'It won't sound any more reasonable to you than it did to Costall.'

'Try me.'

Kirby felt more relaxed than he had done since leaving *Cossack*. Here, in the familiar unit command centre, he could marshall the facts and make an appreciation in curt military shorthand to a man who spoke his language.

When he had finished, Halsall was a half minute before he replied. Then he said, 'I'd go along with that, Grant. You know and I know that we've had to pull them out of trouble before. Wars are fought on pretext not principle. We're in a vicious circle as the Arab proverb has it—No justice without soldiers, no soldiers without money, no money without prosperity, no prosperity without justice. So we keep the peace and get stuck with it and everybody's brickbats for doing it. Well. Get you back to *Cossack* and stay on the station for a spell.

31

Nobody can reach you here. The whole squadron is on stand-by. We're scheduled for escort on this job, so you'll be at hand to see how your friends on Triopus make out. Anything else?'

'No.'

'Take my scout car out to *Cossack* and send it back but quick.'

'What's the big rush?'

'I've been called in to Group HQ for a high level chat. Man called Lasmec. Wilkes has set it up. Thinks I ought to meet one of the top civilian entrepreneurs. Don't worry. I'm not for sale.'

'That I know.'

In his own cabin on *Cossack* the therapy was complete.

On instant blast-off readiness, the ship was a living thing. Wisps of vapour drifted up past his direct vision ports from pre-heating rocket tubes. Standing free of her service gantries, she felt resilient on her hydraulic jacks.

Kirby picked a short, black briar pipe from his locker and enjoyed the ritual of filling it. That again was a special pleasure reserved for landfalls, when a whole natural atmosphere was at hand to supplement the ship's air plant.

It was drawing comfortably when his intercom set up its urgent ping, pitched on orchestral A, and the co-pilot's voice came up from the command cabin.

'Glad to have you back on board, Commander.'

'Thanks, Tom. Hold it. I'll come down.'

In *Cossack*'s small operations room, Captain Tom Mowatt and Bob Scholes, massive tow-haired No. 2 in the power section, looked unaffectedly glad to see him. That was something in its way, since Mowatt had filled the command slot in his absence and might be expected to resent losing control. His first words took any strain out.

'Now perhaps I can get back to my own desk. This centre

console needs an ambidextrous conjuror to man it. It's all yours, Grant, and more than welcome.'

'What's been going on?'

'Routine sheepdog missions in the main. Up and down like a blasted yo-yo. Twice round the gasworks and back home. Those transports wouldn't last a minute if anybody wanted to stop them.

'Nobody would.'

It was inconceivable that deep in the centre of the Galactic Organization's space empire there could be any threat from outside.

'Eastern Hemisphere might try something. Anyway that's the line I got. They'd be glad to delay the project until their own gets under way. There's enough miscellaneous hardware anchored round the freight terminals to build a new planet. You'd see that coming in.'

'No, it was out of phase. we came straight in. Kept on RT right down to re-entry. I'd like to take a look.'

Squadron base link glowed to make a period and Mowatt automatically reached out to take it. Then he remembered and paused. Protocol re-asserted itself. 'It's for *Cossack*, Commander. Will you take it?'

Kirby said, 'Carry on, Captain. I'll listen in.'

A precise female voice came up, relaying a signal from Halsall's command centre. 'Squadron Controller regrets sending *Cossack* out of sequence; but technical faults on *Cougar* have put her out of service for twenty-four hours. Please stand by for routine security checks on freight terminals. Blast off timed for sixteen hundred hours. Acknowledge.'

Again Mowatt looked across at Kirby and this time got briefly, 'Will do.' He said officially to the panel. 'Message received. Timed fourteen-twenty. Commander Kirby has resumed command of *Cossack*. Five minute checks as of now. Out.'

Kirby said, 'So. I get to look at them sooner than I thought.

Okay, Number One, bring in any loose personnel. Briefing fifteen hundred. Sealed up readiness from fifteen-thirty. I'l take a look round the ship.'

First class as Number One, Mowatt had obviously been a good caretaker. In thirty minutes, Kirby went through with a fine-tooth comb and found nothing even marginally below the exacting standards he had himself set. *Cossack* was a taut ship Advanced design, class prototype of a new range of top-size corvettes, overlapping in size and fire power the medium range cruisers, and packing almost twice the power to weight ratio she was a unit to reckon with anywhere in galactic space.

With few changes, he had almost the same crew list. Tague as number one in Navigation, a seasoned spaceman coming up within two years of retirement at the compulsory age of forty eight. Scaiff, at the Power Executive desk, squat, broad shouldered, unshakeable. Massey, top man in communications a slight, spectacled young man still with the same upstanding bristle of ginger hair. Fantastically quick at handling *Cossack'* nerve centre banks of computers.

Their second and third men were unchanged. The new men were concentrated in the general duties section, which meant mainly armament control. All three in this section were replacements. John Sibley, the new exec was an unsmiling man very dark, medium height, contrasting with his two assistant Corness and Devon, who were genial giants and, bulked ou in space gear, went a long way to fill the confined space o their gunnery centre below the cone.

Kirby felt, as usual, the curious detached sense of being both involved and outside the train of events which would bring *Cossack* to the second of blast off. Once the count down pro cedures got under way, there was an inevitability about the end product, which reduced them all to mere robot extension of the computers. No-one in the crowded control cabin could suspect that only half his mind was committed to the spli second responses he was making.

From a vantage point outside himself, he was seeing the slowly turning command island with Mowatt and Tague, left and right, impersonal shrouded figures moving with him in the final check.

Mowatt gathered the reports.

'Navigation all Systems Go,' in a dry, nasal snarl from Tague.

'Power all Systems Go'—clipped and precise from Scaiff.

A pause and then a quick, nervy stammer from Massey, 'Communications. All Systems Go.'

Going by the book, Mowatt handed the data on as though his neighbour had not heard it all on the general net.

'Captain to Commander. All Systems Go.'

A sweep hand on the centre console began to eat into the red quadrant and alarm bleeps picked it up, building tension in the waiting ship.

Then she began to move. Slowly at first. Gathering momentum, with a fireball filling the scanner which had been showing them the pad.

Kirby felt that his watching self and his acting self had slid together like overlapping images in an auto view-finder. Now he was integrated and whole as one man, fully and satisfyingly occupied in conning his ship through the hazards of lift off.

Below them their planet had a jewel glow. Mistily blue. Rivers made ribbons, then strings, then merged into its distant mass. G dropped, and he was free to move, calling for data on an orbit that would bring them round to Number Three Satellite Terminal with its vast concentration of berths and freight sheds.

Central in the complex was the original twenty-first century construction. A cross shaped space station with four huge cans at the arm-ends and a fat central cylinder on a hundred metre diameter. Docking facilities at each free extremity could take ten craft and they were all full. Moored round about and dwarfing the nucleus were twenty of the huge transporters being prepared for the colonization project. Nearby, with flexible connecting chutes, running on universal couplings at the hub, were five wheel-type dormitory blocks. Two supplementary space stations of modern design rode side by side five kilometres out from the old centre.

It looked a fantastic muddle. A labour force of many thousands was on permanent location. Somewhere at the heart of it all was an organizing skill bordering on genius.

Kirby cruised round the perimeter and talked to the duty director. Six of them were taking it round the clock and if the others came up to the same standard, the project would meet its deadlines.

Brought up to twice life-size on the main scanner, Dr Glenn Maynard exuded drive from every photogenic pore. He was about Kirby's age, with a shaven head, smooth-tanned skin and very penetrating grey-flecked eyes. Somewhere along the line, he had accepted the five-star management blueprint—do one thing at a time; know the problem; learn to listen; learn to ask questions; distinguish sense from nonsense. In a short five minute interview, he brought it all into play and Kirby felt that he had been through a suitability-rating session.

But efficiency in others always pleased him, even if he was on the receiving end. When Maynard said that he was going personally with the advance party and was pleased to have had the minority view at first hand, it was a promise at least that whatever was done would be done with full appreciation of all the angles.

It was only when the screen blanked and personality impact was less, that he realized he had heard nothing fresh. Wilkes and Costall, for reasons best known to themselves, just didn't want to know. Maynard would understand all right; but would use the knowledge to make doubly sure there was no slip-up. He was committed to make the Colonization Project go if only as an exercise of professional skill.

Cossack nosed through the tangle at zero thrust, dwarfed by the immense, lumpy dormitory cans. They would end up in

36

permanent orbit round Triopus. Ready-made to form its first satellite stations. Since they would never meet an atmosphere, aerodynamics had no part in design. They were ugly and functional, with built-on accretions for all the possible uses they would have.

Docking collars at every conceivable angle showed that escorting ships would be expected to nose in and shove, if ever a course correction had to be made. They would get an initial send-off from the space terminal, calculated to bring them to the gravisphere of Triopus, and small booster motors would help out; but the powered ships in the convoy would have a full-time job to keep them in line and nurse them into an orbit at journey's end.

An Eastern Hemisphere freighter flashed briefly into view and disappeared, making for the Cathay Terminal. Kirby pulled out and continued his tour.

It was twenty-three hundred precisely on the clock when *Cossack* flexed down on her jacks and the gantries crept in under billowing clouds of coolant to damp out thermal glow.

Block house desk had an urgent memo. 'Commander Kirby to report at once to Squadron Control.'

Kirby took his scout car, with one of the new men, Pete Corness, humped hugely over the miniature console. When he reached the Centre, there was an orderly waiting to take him through. 'Squadron Controller Halsall is waiting to see you, Commander.'

That was something in itself. Halsall must have come in specially for it. What was it then? A hatchet job? Wilkes and Co. able to get their own way even here?

Halsall was sitting at his desk as though he had never left it.

'Come in, Grant. Come in. Now hear this. When you talked to me before, I believed you; but to be honest I thought you were on the wrong tack. Political matters are not our business. However, Wilkes has been trying to get me to take you off the active list. He wouldn't dream that up all by himself. I think a man I met called Lasmec has a big say in this. Now, I reckon, if they're that keen, there must be a lot in what you say. They want a corvette for the advance party and it's due out this day week. So it's *Cossack*. Okay? That'll teach Wilkes to try his intrigue on my squadron. What do you say? It means another long spell without leave.'

Kirby said, 'Can they get at you?"

'I'll worry about that. At the moment I've promised a ship. They'll have the name when it's too late to change. Check?'

'Check.'

There was a logic about it. Kirby felt that he had known from the start that he would see Triopus again from the deck of his own ship.

Chapter Three

Grant Kirby looked out of the direct vision port of his cabin and thought again that the huge lumbering tank on his port quarter was an insult to the orderly beauty of space.

Even the incredible technical achievement of its blast-off from Terminal Three, in no way compensated for its presence among the stars. It was an eyesore, a monstrosity.

Farther aft, he could see the probing cone of *Europa 12*, one of the two civilian freight and exploration ships which made up the convoy. *Philadelphia*, the other ship, was out of sight on the far side of the gas plant.

As he watched, the mountain of metal completed a slow turn and brought its nameplate into view. Letters three metres high. *New World*. For his money it should have read MAMMON.

Dr Glen Maynard was installed behind an executive desk on the transport as representative of the civil arm and first director of the fledgling colony. Hadden was along as adviser. Martinez with his staff were scheduled for the main party.

Recriminations had been quick, but brief. There was no doubt that Maynard had his number from Lasmec, but he had to admit the man made a quick recovery. Personnel management skills bubbled to the top. Kirby was here present and had to be integrated in the master plan.

One thing Kirby had made clear. Whatever authority the governor-designate might wield on Triopus, there was only one controller in deep space. The commander of *Cossack* was charged with responsibility for the safe arrival of the convoy into the gravisphere of the planet and the navigational directives would come from the corvette.

At first, the civilian ships had tailed out in line astern; but Kirby had seen that any quick shift to be worked on *New World* would need them both handily placed to slip into its docking collars. Seconds could be saved. He sent out a signal telling them to a fraction where to sail.

Neither moved. *Cossack* swept round, cleared for action and threatened to convert *Europa* into molecular scrap. Kirby's face coming up on every scanner was living proof that he meant no less. When he began to count down there was an instant shuffle round.

Without doubt, he was the most unpopular man in the convoy.

In *New World* talk on the thronged mess decks was indignant.

'Fascist.'

'Whose side is that bastard on?'

'Military swine. They'd like to have everybody in a uniform.'

'Power mad. We've drawn a right one there. He's the one who wanted to stop the project. Paid agitator. Somebody in Eastern got to him with a backhander. Beats me why the government put him on this detail.'

But signals from *Cossack* were obeyed. Commanders of the freight ships saw the point and recognized his professionalism, but used to taking an independent line they resented loss of freedom.

Fifty days out and they had reason to be thankful that *Cossack* was in the party.

Kirby woke at the first bleep of the alarm in his cabin roof.

'Commander.'

Tague's voice came up harsh and matter-of-fact.

'Unidentified objects coming from dead ahead. Very fast. Could be two ships.'

'Call stations.'

'Check.'

Urgent bleeps sounded through *Cossack*. Kirby was coming

through the hatch into his control cabin on the tenth beat, visor still hinged back.

'What do you make of it, Carl?'

'Two for sure. Coming up fast.'

'What time have we got?'

'Ten minutes. Maybe twelve. There's a lot of loose light.'

'Get me on general net.'

Kirby spoke direct to duty officers. 'Hear this. Craft coming up on course could be hostiles. *Europa* and *Philadelphia* take up positions in docking collars. It may be necessary to manoeuvre the can out of line of fire. Action Stations.'

Even in haste, he could not dignify the hulk with a ship's name.

He saw *Europa* move in and took *Cossack* in a tight roll so that he was symmetrically placed above the composite creature that evolved.

Massey, juggling with a mounting pile of data was ready with a judgement. Cutting procedure, he fairly spluttered into his mike.

'Definitely two. Collision course. High density.'

Kirby thought, 'So this is it. No Western units on this tack. Not freight. Must be military. Between them they'll carve that heap into shreds.'

Aloud he said, 'Convoy leader to *Europa*. Major course change. Full thrust. Now.'

It was very hard on the huddled masses in *New World*. Unless they had moved smartly to action stations there would be a considerable run on hospitalization when the action was over. If they were still sentient enough to demand it. Anybody out of an acceleration couch would have to take a thousand kilos of pressure wherever he happened to be.

The mass disappeared from beneath his keel as though by sleight of hand and *Cossack* was alone on the original course.

Now he could see the approaching ships as discrete specks

41

of hurrying light. Well-spaced. They would take *Cossack* from either side.

Still there was no recognition signal. No response to the galactic code queries Mowatt was throwing out. 'What ships? Why are you on this course? What are your intentions?'

That was a stupid one. Anyone having to be asked would hardly say, 'honourable'.

There was also the point that they were giving unnecessary advantages to a hostile to pinpoint *Cossack* by her own signal beam.

Kirby said, 'Hold fast on that Number One.'

There were three minutes in it. Then two and there was no doubt about the ships. Corvette size, but with an unfamiliar run of line that nobody could identify. Blue black, without markings of any kind. Long probing antennae, from many-facetted cones like blown up segments of a wasp's eye.

Kirby held on. Then he snapped down on the link from Massay which was working the ship on computerized data. He had it on manual and dropped them in a sickening roll which took them to the limit of G tolerance.

Overhead two livid lines seared out and met in an incandescent asterisk at the spot where *Cossack* should have been.

All doubt was gone. There was satisfaction in that, but it was short-lived. Out of the tail of his eye, Kirby saw one ship peel off in a tight curve to follow the convoy.

It was a bitter minute. After all his big brother act, when it came right down to it, he could not even protect the civilians. Before they went under they would be right to curse him as a useless big mouth.

Even as the thought crossed his mind, he was pulling *Cossack* round and taking her in a climbing turn which would give Sibley's gunners a chance.

For a second, he had lost the black craft; then it was underneath them and near enough to hit with a half brick. There was an instant's view along its length and a glimpse down

42

through a direct vision port with a visor turning to look up. No visible face. It might have been an empty suit. *Cossack*'s main armament delivered with a surge that threw them momentarily into sideways slip.

Kirby did not bother to look. No metal known to man could have survived that broadside. He was pulling *Cossack* round in a bid to catch the second craft before it could lock on the mass of *New World*.

Watchers on the hulk saw that he had an impossible task. Unable to move, they could only wait, classical, inertial observers, while a malevolent blue-black streak picked up the new course and came on.

Maynard, driving like a slaver, got the last collision bulkhead sealed off before the first beam struck home.

Sheer bulk became a protective factor. With the best will in the world the attacking pilot needed time to carve it up. A ten-metre swathe in the stern bared the innards of the tank. Compartments opened up like a shattered house in an earthquake. Debris tumbled out. A man holding a grip making an illogical effort at flight.

Then the stranger was past and turning to run in again. *Cossack* appeared, a rising sun over the arc of the vast cylinder.

Sibley was waiting with everything trained forward.

It could still have been too late; but the oncoming pilot had a change of mind. He began a suicide dive for the centre of *New World*. The hesitation cost him a nonasecond and Kirby was on to him like a striking hawk.

Fragments of the distintegrating craft sheered off a docking collar and left long streaks of shining, incandescent metal in arcs on the hull.

New World absorbed the energy in a frenetic roll and she was still spinning wildly when Kirby brought *Cossack* back in station and began calling for corrective thrust from the freighters.

In three minutes they were stable, in space as empty as it

had ever been, with only a tangle of wreckage as living proof that an attack had been made.

Maynard came up, face set and grey with strain, but still topped up with managerial zeal. 'Did you identify those craft, Commander?'

Kirby said shortly, 'Not listed in any recognition manual. Report casualties.'

'Checks are not complete. Many men housed in sector T, had not reached it when the bulkheads closed. Most of those are injured.'

This last was an oblique gripe at the course change which had been rushed on him.

Kirby said, 'No doubt they'd rather be injured than dead. As of now, collision hatches will be on permanent seal.'

'That will make movement very difficult. Perhaps you are not aware that assembly work is going on all the time? There is a deadline to meet.'

It was a nice opening for sarcasm; but Kirby had no wish to score points. He said, 'Nevertheless, the drill must be followed. Handling characteristics will be affected by that rubble aft. Do you need help to clear it away?'

'No. We can manage that.'

'Very well. I shall come across and inspect.'

There was little pleasure in the prospect as far as Maynard's expression went. Clearly, he believed that his complement of riggers could handle it without help from the military arm. But he managed a curt agreement.

'Sector L lock then.'

Kirby took Bob Scholes, his Power Number 2, who had proved in the past to have a considerable flair for improvization.

With *Cossack* pacing twenty metres from the can, they waited on the step for its slow spin to bring the lock round.

It was like facing a moving wall. Usually in space Kirby was conscious of distance and a kind of all-round pull towards disintegration of the spirit. As though only the tough fabric of his suit was holding him together as a single unit. That he might expand and fill the universe like a gas. This time he felt diminished by the impending bulk of *New World*.

He counted the gaunt, descending girder ribs to establish a time sequence and, with the lock high above them, called, 'Now.'

Small launching jets from *Cossack* shot them across the gap with a split second to uncouple spring-loaded lines and latch on to mooring rings.

Cossack disappeared round the twist. After the speed of their action the wait for attention from the porter stretched out as an eternity of time to match the infinity of space behind them. When the outer hatch began to peel back, it was as though they were being given grudging entry to a holy mountain.

Scholes grumbled, 'They take their time.'

Even inside, the welcome was less than incandescent. Each entry port on *New World* had a wide reception area which doubled as recreation space for its sector. Currently it was in use as a casualty clearing centre and its couches were lined up as in a hospital ward.

At full stretch, the medical unit of two doctors and twenty nursing sisters had set up a similar bay in every sector. Here, two nurses, helped by the two stand-by men from the lock gear, were working methodically through a waiting list of thirty odd. Fractures mainly, from taking pressure wherever they had happened to fall.

Most of them had not done the sum and sorted out what the recent action had been all about. For their money it was more evidence of high-handed military intervention. News of the damage to *New World* had not been relayed to all sectors.

Kirby, visor hinged back, said, 'Where do I find Maynard?'

The nearer nurse took time off from spraying a quick-set cast to give him a tight-lipped grimace compounded of professional welcome and 'I-set-'em-up-you-knock-'em-down'.

She said, 'I need the men here. *Dr* Maynard is in the control centre. Do you know the way?'

An attention ping from the tannoy made a period. A very cool and familiar voice came up calling the score. More contralto through the electronic filter, but definitely Rapunzel her own self. 'The emergency is over. *New World* has sustained damage in Sector T. All riggers in Sectors D and E are to assemble in Sector E Reception and draw space gear. Mr Ramsden will be in charge of the combined party. Dr Maynard is making a personal inspection of every sector. Any loss to individual property will be made good from the colony store.'

She ceased. It was well received. Maynard's public relations team were working overtime.

That was more than could be said for internal circulation. Delays at every collision hatch, with a stage wait before an operator could be found to clear the inner seals, kept Kirby in mounting impatience for thirty-five minutes by his time disk before they were through to Sector A and the vast observation and control deck of the transport.

Twice he called *Cossack* for information. Nothing was stirring. Seemingly the two craft were alone. But to find the convoy in an infinity of space time they must have had precise knowledge of course data.

Kirby spent some of his dead time thinking it out. If they were scouting craft from a larger force, they would hardly have gone into an attack. It would have been enough to sheer off and report. The once-and-for-all suicide bid of the second craft was in its way a guarantee that they were alone.

On the other hand, if the information was available to them, it was available to others. He ruled out Eastern altogether. The project was not liked there, but they would hardly push it to an issue which would bring war. Against all reason, he was forced to believe that they were from Triopus. But it was a view which, this time, he would keep to himself. Nothing he had seen there made it feasible. No evidence

46

collected by the first expedition. They could only wait.

Meanwhile, he would see Maynard and then get off a private signal to Halsall, which would alert the squadron when the main party set out.

Governor-designate Maynard had recovered his urbanity. Whatever damage had been done in the vast oval control room had been put right. He was standing on the raised observation deck with a small knot of advisers all in space gear with visors hinged back ready to go out on their flag-showing tour.

Fifty metres of curving panoramic windshield made a star map back-drop. Kirby came up from the huddle of operating consoles in the well by a broad stairway like the processional way of a ziggurat. A blonde head with its hank of hair dropping mysteriously into a corrugated silver suit turned to see him in. This time, identification was easy. An oblong panel on her chest told all.

It said, 'Logistics: Dr Barbara Hulse.' Her face, framed by the clutter of gear, looked younger and more vulnerable. Her eyes were brown. That was unexpected. He has assumed they were blue. It gave her person a warmer glow.

At this point, field study was interrupted by Maynard who spun sharply on his heel and said, 'Ah, Commander, I'm glad you are here at last. You can accompany us on a tour of the sectors.'

On his left was another old buddy. Mark Hadden, side burns in impeccable trim, said, 'It looks as though somebody doesn't like us, Commander.'

Kirby said, 'The purity of our intentions must be its own reward. Let's go then.'

Watching Maynard in action, was an eye-opener for simple military men. In Sector D, Scholes said, 'That man just isn't true. If this was a family group they'd be bringing babies out for him to touch.'

'Don't forget he's got a very talented public relations crew image-building for him. It wouldn't surprise me if they were

47

putting out subliminal feeds on the closed-circuit video.'

'Pictures of our hero patting an injured dog infiltrating the subconscious.'

'Something like that.'

They had fallen back in the column and Maynard was going through his patter as convincingly as though it was all spontaneous stuff which had bubbled from a full heart at the sight of his suffering people.

Behind them, Barbara Hulse, who managed to walk with a light step even clad in complete steel said indignantly, 'I am surprised to hear you say that, Commander Kirby. It shows a poor spirit. Doctor Maynard is an excellent leader. I admire him for it.'

It was true too. There was a flush of colour along her cheek-bones and an embattled light in her brown eyes.

Kirby said, 'I didn't know you were there. You may be right. It just seems a little contrived.' It was pacifically said with apology in the tone, but appeasement was a non-starter.

'Anyone as gifted as yourself in rousing antagonism would naturally be jealous of such a personality.'

He let it ride. The circus was, anyway, on the move. They filed through into Sector E and had it all over again.

Damage was superficial. Loose gear, not adequately chocked off, had run amok and made a bid for the great outside. Men caught at an angle had broken bones. Miraculously the only dead were in Sector T.

Kirby finally had enough. He said, 'I see the pattern. We have been very lucky. I'll join the repair team for a spell and then get back to my ship.'

Maynard, happy in his work, took the loss to his entourage without visible grief. 'Very well, Commander.' Since he was in the groove for spreading sweetness and light, he also added, belatedly, 'Thank you for your prompt action. We owe you a great deal.'

Hadden had disappeared, showing unusual independence of spirit on his part.

Outside, the maintenance gang had already stripped away much of the debris. Some had already been kicked free with a divergent thrust to send it on an independent career in space for an eternity of wandering. Kirby was in time to stop the launching of a twenty metre block of rubble.

As a professional, he saw the multiplication of space hazards as a stupidity. He said, 'Hold fast with that. Cut it into billets and take it inside.'

Ramsden said, 'That will take time. We have a schedule to meet.'

'Tether it if you like and work on it in your own time; but loose in space that could wreck a ship. How many dead?'

Ramsden said, 'This way,' and they worked through a tangle of twisted girders to a clear space sticking out like a shelf from the wall of the Sector S.

Opaque, green-plastic disposal bags had been used. Laid out in a row there were twenty-eight.

'That's all we found. Maybe one or two fell away.'

Kirby reflected that they ought to be taken inside to a destructor, but it would be bad for morale to have corpses moved through the ship. He said, 'All identified?'

'Yes. I've got coded bracelets from everyone.'

'Rope them together then and launch them out. *Cossack* can deal with it.'

Ramsden's agreement sounded like relief. He had not relished the idea of playing mortician.

When the string of oblong packages trailed out like a chunky jade necklace, Kirby called Mowatt. 'Slip back and neutralize that lot, Tom, or some lucky traveller might collect it like a *leis*.'

The long line was dwindling astern when *Cossack* came round, a lean silver shape, and ran briefly along its length.

A brilliant blue glow ravelled back the thread and the packages were gone. A poor equivalent to the weighted bier slipping overside to the shrill of pipes and definitely setting the First Cause a major problem for any resurrection ploy.

Kirby, watching from an empty bay which had been a cubicle cabin for one of them thought bitterly that the complex structure of a man deserved a better fate. Even here in the ultimate nowhere, there should have been some break in the silence, some sign that their human span had not been as pointless as it was made to appear. The dispersed molecular trash they had become, could have disposed itself into the words 'Goodbye, then' before it hurried off as a speck of energy in the gaseous centre of a new star.

This high-level train of introspection came near to being his last.

Scholes was working out of sight, with a gang which had got on to the main cargo hold of the sector.

Central in the mass, it could be retained as a projecting boss. He was explaining to the foreman an idea for bolting on certain girders which could be led back, clad with salvaged plating and made into an access corridor. It was a project which would take time, but would save endless trouble for the rest of the trip.

Kirby had hooked himself to a ring bolt in the bulkhead behind him and moved out to the lip of the shelf for an unrestricted view aft. He felt a tiny vibration in the deck when the shackle dropped free.

He was manoeuvering round to check out the action when hands seized each arm and launched him in the wake of *Cossack* where her superheated trail was set up to do a neat cremating job.

Before his feet had well cleared the deck, he was grabbing for the flare pistol in his belt.

Whoever had seized the chance had not thought it out far enough. The civilian suits of the riggers were equipped with spring-loaded tethers, but not the comprehensive tool sets of the military pattern. With thirty metres of space between himself and the transport, Kirby had worked himself round and was ready to jet back.

The whole after-end of *New World* was in view. He could see the platform he had launched from, empty now, with no-one even near it and groups of men all diligent and full of virtue. He saw Scholes in grey gear, and the other figures working over the rim from the lock in Sector S. Maynard and his party on the last leg of their mission.

Barbara Hulse's corrugated silver suit was third in line and he saw the visor turn and look out to where he was. Then she was tapping her neighbour to draw attention to the man doing tricks in the outback.

Grant Kirby came in like a bulbous quarrel bolt and fended off just below Hadden, hooking on to a ring and taking up the recoil on his spring-ratchet line.

He grabbed Hadden's communication link and plugged in.

Hadden was too ready with a question. 'Unseen enemies again, Commander? I shouldn't make too much of it. It sounds like persecution complex. They'll think you've been in space too long. The Governor could have you relieved of your command as medically unfit.'

Kirby said, 'I'm getting very tired of it, Hadden. Let's put it this way. If there's a next time, I'll come looking for you. Make no mistake about that.'

'If there's a next time the chances are you won't be in a position to go looking for anybody.'

Maynard came up on the radio link. 'Marsden tells me you've cleared out the casualties. You should have referred that to me. I had decided to have a simple commemorative ceremony. The men would like to know that the occasion was properly honoured.'

'Which men?'

'You know what I mean, Commander. What were you doing out there?'

51

Kirby was suddenly sick of the whole business. He said, 'I was checking the trim. *New World* is all right. Remember the drill for keeping all internal hatches closed.'

The owner of the silver suit was hanging on to a projecting loop of debris in spite of the security of a safety line clipped to a ring bolt. Something in the lines of the figure, even when in near total anonymity, suggested strain. When her visor came round and he could look through to a set pale face, he knew that she was having to force herself to keep up with the column. Her eyes were nearly all pupil with a ring of rich brown.

Superimposed on the bulky suit as though looking at an infra-red spectrograph he had a momentary flashback to her early-morning appearance in her doorway.

Emotion had made her ultra-sensitive and her eyes told him, through two windows and a metre of vacuum, that she had recognized his flight of fancy. Difficult though the feat was in the circumstances, she made a small gesture which had all the impact of a musical-comedy toss of the head. An actress in the grand manner lost to the boards.

When she spoke it was to Maynard, with formality in view of the other ears on the net, but with a timbre in the rich contralto which hinted intimacy. 'There is nothing for me to do here, Dr Maynard. I'll go back and get on with the manifest. There are some alterations to make.'

His reply was casually authoritative. 'Do that, Barbara. We'll be through in half an hour.'

He had not seen or did not care that she was frightened.

Kirby said, 'I'll get back to my ship,' and moved off behind her, calling Scholes on the way.

She had some trouble at the rim, where a flange of metal stuck out like a cornice and there was nothing for it but to work round for a couple of metres without a hook holding. When she stopped, he said, 'Go ahead. I'll hold you.'

When the door of S lock sliced behind her, she had not spoken, nor did she look round again, but the dark night of space seemed more oppressive when she had gone.

Mowatt had been on to Galactic Control. Nothing was known of any hostiles within light years of the convoy's path. No registered military craft from any planet tallied with the description he had given.

Kirby said, 'That's okay as far as it goes, but they and we both know, that not every inhabited planet has been checked out. There are still as many unknown as known.'

'But they wouldn't know the course we were on and come right in.'

'No, they wouldn't know that.'

'Look, Grant. It couldn't be Lasmec. Why would he want to louse up his own project?'

'That only leaves Triopus itself.'

'So?'

'You've seen the tapes.'

It was a debate that went on at intervals through the long weeks of the mission.

Routine settled to its deep space rhythm. In the middle passage they were out of touch even by the faint attenuated signals of the Galactic Organization itself. A hurrying world of their own going nowhere from nowhere.

On *New World*, work details went on round the clock. Reentry capsules were filled with pre-fabricated building sections ready to be launched through the atmosphere of Triopus. Towards the end, redeployment of inner spaces in the ship itself was begun to fit it for its long-term role as part of a satellite complex.

Grant Kirby spent two days in Maynard's personnel office, checking profiles. Wasted labour; there was nothing to suggest that any men had affiliation with any organization. Recordswise they were clean as a hound's tooth.

Here and there he found faces which reminded him of other

security files. Hard to isolate just where it lay, but he memorized them and the names.

On Barbara Hulse's card he saw the declaration that her uncle on her mother's side was one Oskar Lasmec. That explained a good deal. Her list of academic qualifications was formidable. Like Maynard she had picked up a doctorate in Science.

He went through the transport, taking time in every sector until he had visited each working party. Maynard protected his image by sending one of his staff tagging along to give the tours an air of official sanction. Once he drew Hadden, once it was Barbara Hulse.

Hadden said as they went round a close-packed engineering shop, 'Anybody giving a guilty start here, Commander, would get himself diced by a power take-off.'

'Don't tempt me, Hadden.'

'That's all right, Commander; it's just as well I appreciate your refined humour.'

Kirby was hardly listening as he took in detail of the two dozen men working round him, checking off names from identity tags against a nominal roll he had prepared. Only one of those present had an asterisk against him. There were twenty such in the list that he wanted to look at more closely. He had a useful flair for memorizing faces, though some mug shots in the record were up to two years old.

Hadden, anxious to make his point, went on, 'Yes, we shall be working closely together. As you will understand, there is a constitution for the new colony which gives the governor control of armed forces. Once on the planet, Dr Maynard will be legally your C-in-C. Of course, he will be too busy to take personal charge and he has delegated the department to me. Defence Minister, you might say.'

Kirby had found the man he was looking for. A small, ferret-faced surly character in the white coveralls of a foreman. But

54

Hadden got an audience at last when the implications filtered home.

'We shall just have to hope, for your sake, that the job stays a sinecure.'

Then he edged through a narrow corridor of stacked gear and spoke to the foreman. 'Keeping up to schedule, Lomax?'

Use of the name surprised the man into civility. 'That's right, Commander.' Then he looked over Kirby's shoulder to Hadden with an unspoken question.

Hadden said, 'The Commander is very interested in you, Lomax. You'll have to watch it or you'll be press-ganged into the navy.'

'I'll watch it, and that's a fact.'

Barbara Hulse took the opportunity for a display of expertise, appearing for the chore in trim green coveralls with an intricate monogram in gold wire on the ogee arch of her left breast pocket. Hair intricately piled in pale swathes. Whether it was to counter-weight her showing as an astronaut or whether it was just automatic efficiency, she allowed no time for personal chat. When the tour was finished he was no nearer being a friend of her bosom.

One thing was clear. Maynard had not brought her along for the ride, there was no detail of supply down to the last self-tapping screw which was outside the reach of her busy fingers.

Good fingers at that. Long and shapely with oval nails that ran down a manifest with an authoritative tap. Wasted on the governor-designate's shaven head, Kirby thought.

In fact, it was beginning to annoy him, that one with such potential as a honey should be so consumed with a passion for inanimate objects. And for his money it was a class rating which included Maynard.

Looking across from *Cossack*, when his mind shifted into

neutral after a navigational ploy, he found he was thinking more and more about the Maynard/Hulse setup and not liking it. He told himself that free will was for all. She was old enough to know what she was doing. What *was* she doing at this moment of time though, across the vacuum strip, deep in the convoluted heart of *New World?*

It was easy to fall into the universal error of supposing that in the next street, life moved at a better rhythm. The mystical 'there', where the great, illuminating action was.

Kirby had told himself that for those who were 'there', 'here' itself was 'there'. The philosophical implication of it carried him into the depths of his own mind like a visitor.

The alarm pinger in his cabin roof was making a third strike before he surfaced and said harshly, 'Kirby.'

Mowat said, 'There's the beginning of a reading. Gravisphere of Triopus coming up.'

Chapter Four

On Day 107, hitting the precise deadline, the convoy swept into the positive gravitational field of the green planet. Kirby had the three, powered ships nosed into collars on the huge disk of *New World*'s prow and warped her back out of counterpoint in a blaze of retro.

Saucer size on the scanners, Triopus glowed like a flat jewel on a black velvet show pad. Four moons, silver beads in a tetrahedron.

Kirby swivelled slowly on his command island, feeling a sense of anticlimax. After the attack in deep space, he had expected opposition. What form it would take he could not tell, but it would not have surprised him to find a screen of fighters arrowing up to meet them.

When it came, it was simpler. Massey stopped calling course data and said, 'Disregard that Commander. Re-check.'

Five seconds later with the composite craft on the first leg of an equilateral spiral, he said apologetically, 'No dice. I'll check again.'

Kirby was glad to find that he made no hesitation. It was a bitter decision, to call for help to a civilian ship, but personal issues never clouded judgement, 'Call *Europa*. Ask for confirmation.'

Massey spoke to his opposite number and there was as much relief as surprise in his next transmission. '*Europa* has the same bug.'

'Try *Philadelphia*.'

A full minute was eaten away before Massey had it established. Even the massive computer array on *New World* was punching out gibberish.

Now they had flattened out into a dive for Triopus and acceleration was building in logarithmic progression.

Kirby's mind was racing to process data. *Cossack* alone would be straightforward to take on manual, but with the clumsy can and the offset freighters, there was a set of handling characteristics which would task the computers.

On the general net, he called all commanders. 'Ground interference. I'll call the shots. As of now. Half retro *Europa*. Number one, take *Cossack* out and re-engage aft of Sector K.'

It was a lonely duel, in which nobody could help. Working with a triangle of forces and with only a rough knowledge of what he could draw in power from the freighters, the first half minute was trial and error. Error which for one dizzy spell sent *New World* into an offbeat corkscrew spin.

He had time to wonder how Barbara Hulse was making out as a lay figure on an acceleration couch in the whirling operations room. But it was thinking at a level which did not check the working surface of his mind.

Reaction times came into it. His own and the executives' on the freighters. He came to appreciate that *Philadelphia* delivered fractionally later than *Europa* and had to allow for it. Whether or not they ought to be there at all, no longer bothered him. It was a straightforward professional job.

When the satellite levelled off in orbital flight, Triopus was filling the scanner, continents and oceans in clear detail. He held them at stations for a full circuit, an hour and twenty minutes by the clock, steadying, finally, until they were in a parking orbit above the centre of the largest land mass, a familiar landmark. Now they kept pace with the revolution of the planet. He said, 'That's it. Stabilize there. Stand down. Stay on instant recall.'

Hadden's voice came up to make a period. A general broadcast to all hands. 'We have arrived at journey's end. Governor Maynard wishes to put on record a personal message for every man.'

It was hardly possible for anyone with a shaven head and dedicated self-interest to look benevolent; but Maynard had the right form of words. He went to the taproots of human motivation. The aggressive drive to have and hold a piece of land; the need to think that a course of action was as noble as it was expedient, the desire for security for a family group. He ended with a sentimental toast, calling them all so many Conquistadores landing now on a New World full of promise.

Twice life size on the scanner in *Cossack*, his head dwarfed the planet itself.

Kirby had stayed on duty in his control cabin. Visor hinged back, he was completing his log of the day's work. He was struck by the discrepancy between the words from the throne and the appearance of the speaker. Maynard's eyes were not committed to what he was saying and his even tone would have been equally suited to a meteorology newscast.

Probably he hadn't written it anyway. It smacked of the PR staff with perhaps the fine feminine hand of Barbara Hulse putting in a line.

When it was done there was a direct call to *Cossack*. Hadden again, very smug. 'The Governor is holding an executive. There's a lot of detail to finalize. I'll see you over here in fifteen minutes, Commander Kirby.'

Defence Minister rank had settled already on his ever-willing shoulders.

Mowat said, 'We've drawn one there all right. What did we ever do for this?'

Kirby said, 'When I'm clear, pull out and give yourself room. Watch the land and blast anything that moves this way. I'll call in, when I want to be taken off.'

'Watch yourself.'

'I'll do that.'

Waiting for A Sector lock to open, Kirby saw dark, racing shadows eat into the sphere below, as it turned away from the sun.

Night on this hemisphere of Triopus. Scented and languorous; resinous wood fires in the houses; soft light of torches which burned without smoke. Thin high music on a pentatonic scale which seemed to suggest an air without precise definition and left the listener wanting to hear more. Slender, graceful people, living without urgency.

Technically backward by Earth's measure. But civilized. Certainly civilized. How would they cope with Maynard and his menagerie? Why, when you got right down to it, should they have to try?

The first Gubernatorial Council was set with a sense of occasion on the observation platform. Like Banquo's ghost, Kirby was one by himself, being the only person present still in space gear.

They were waiting for him. Ten in all, eleven when he had lumbered into the empty seat. At the head, Maynard was in full dress as a top-rank rep of the Colonization Ministry. White, high-necked tunic with gold buttons carrying a Western Hemisphere map in bas-relief. Blue epaulettes with the same motif. On the right, Hadden, in black, with a cluster of three silver stars on his right shoulder.

Kirby recognized the senior medico, two PR men, a production expert, a surveyor and accepted the rest without identification when his roving eye fell on Barbara Hulse.

His empty seat was at the bottom of the board facing up to Maynard. She was half way down on the left. Quarter profile watching the chairman. Cadmium yellow tabard with bare arms and considerable gusset interest. Hair falling back in a pale elastic curtain from a white head band of electrum set with amethysts. Curve of cheekbone and chin making a satisfying mathematical statement against the offset cylinder throat.

This aesthetic holiday ended abruptly with Maynard's opening sally. 'Although this is a formal meeting, the first of the Governing Council for Triopus, to mark our arrival at journey's end, there is also a piece of necessary business.'

60

He picked a clear plastic document case from the table and held it up. Large blue and white seals marked its official Western Hemisphere legality. Bottom right, a black and gold stamp showed that the Galactic Organization had given it the okay. No assent from Triopus was visible; but listening to the rolling jargon, it seemed to suggest that all and sundry were bending backward to do them a big favour.

Kirby, for the exercise, translated it into basic speech tones, the Galactic lingua franca, which had been devised by the linguists for Communication wherever a culture had developed the spoken word.

Stripped of its round-about phraseology, it came down to a simple declaration of theft. There was some lofty stuff about the indivisibility of man wherever he lived in the galaxy and the rights he had to take empty lands for his use. There was not much about his right to the simple life. In fact it was specifically stated that he had a duty to carry the fruits of his technical advance and make them available to his neighbour. Whether this was necessarily an act of love was nowhere defined.

When it was done, Maynard was, officially, all there was of power in Triopus. His first act was symbolic. Ancient fertility rite. He said, 'As the chief magistrate I have the power to grant pairing applications. When the main force arrives there will be an opportunity for all. However I will announce now the first partnership for the eugenic records of the colony. Myself and Dr Barbara Hulse. The official ceremony will be held as soon as the governor's lodge has been built.'

So. A dynastic union. Lasmec had a family link with this outpost of his commercial empire. Kirby watched for some reaction from the girl; but there was none. No blush of pleasure or pallor of dismay. Treated as a business arrangement? She was looking thinner than when he had seen her before. Working hard no doubt.

There was a round of applause from the meeting and some

toilers in the well below lifted their head from their consoles to see what was going on at the high table.

There was nothing much to see. Maynard sat tight making no move to bring his consort-elect to his side. Nor did she, seemingly, expect it. She put on a standard congratulation-receiving smile, looked briefly round the circle and went on checking out data on the pad in front of her.

Not the behaviour of a Heloise or an Iseult. Kirby was surprised to find that he was sorry for her. It was not like that with the people of Triopus. There an engagement was a pretext for elaborate celebrations and the couple at the centre radiated delight.

Maynard passed quickly to the next business. He read slowly and clearly the section of the constitution relating to Military Forces.

'There shall be established a Military Staff Committee which shall consist of the Governor or his representative as Chairman, two members of the Governing Council and the Commander of all military units in the area. This committee shall be responsible for carrying out the policy of the Governing Council. Except where purely military strategy is concerned it has no power of initiation in itself.'

Maynard stopped and looked down the table at Kirby. 'As the only military commander in the area, you are a member of this Staff Committee, Commander. Later, of course, it will be the Commander-in-Chief of all units present. My office will be represented by Controller Hadden. I suggest, as the other members, Dr Hulse—whose knowledge of logistics would always be valuable and Sub-Controller Rosencrat, who can handle the public relations aspects. But I think it is sufficiently clear that only this body is able to decide on a course of action. There is no danger that the Military Staff Committee will start or indeed stop a war off its own bat. Only decisions of the Governing Council will be carried out by the Military Staff Committee.'

Kirby recognized that the point was being laboured for his benefit. He raised his right hand like a voter. After all the rolling, legalistic phrases, his laconic acceptance produced a palpable temperature drop. 'I get the message. You tell me. I do it.'

Barbara Hulse's head came round for a direct look and he saw that her face was indeed thinner and her brown eyes seemed larger by comparison.

Kirby went on, 'Perhaps some mathematical genius will tell me how to calculate for a landfall without using computerized data. Unless we can get down there, the new colony is committed to life as a satellite economy. I don't have to tell you that we cannot mount a launching device here to send *New World* back.'

Hadden said, 'That is a pessimistic view, Commander. There will be no question of sending *New World* back. The difficulties are purely temporary. There is nothing to stop *Cossack* going down. She can make it clear that the interference with our computers must cease or retributive measures will be taken.

'Such as?'

'This is just the sort of item which would be better ironed out in the Military Staff Committee.'

'Why? The responsibility will have to be shared by the whole administration.'

Maynard said with a kind of icy patience, 'You are being naïve about this, Commander. You have been on missions before when you have had to take punitive action against a hostile population.'

Ten pairs of eyes had now tracked round to the troll in the fancy dress. Only one set, brown and considering, interested him at all. He made his explanatory gloss direct to them.

'Hostiles have been defined as those outside the reach of intelligent co-operation as outlined in the Galactic Code. Here we have intelligent and cultured beings who are saying that they don't want to be colonized.'

63

Her reply was on the official line; but the warmth of her husky contralto took the edge from it. Also there, a tiny element of self doubt in the background. A new thing. Perhaps a hundred days close to Maynard was making a mark.

She said, '*You* say that, Commander. I have no doubt that you believe your opinion to be true. But an official commission has reported on this. We must act on a majority decision. Enough people on Triopus accepted the project. Law is on our side. You need have no misgivings about using force.'

'Suppose, just suppose, I go along with that. Who do I go and see down there? There is no local government as far as we know. Local groups manage their own affairs. Threatening to wipe out one small community isn't going to influence the whole planet.'

Maynard said, 'That again is your impression. There must be a central government, however loose its reins are. They'll know soon enough, if you put down a short term radiation grid. Whatever you have to do, must be done quickly. It will be very bad for morale, if the advance party is hung up here. There is nothing further for the Governing Council.' He turned to Hadden, 'I suggest you carry on now in your office and work out a task detail for the military support unit.'

Kirby, trudging along as last man in the quartet, found himself two paces behind the first-lady designate. Loss of a kilo or so had given her waist a sharper definition. A faint scent of sandalwood beat the air-change mechanism and reached out to him.

He said, as though carrying on a conversation, 'When you see them you'll know what I mean.' Then he carried on, into unchartered waters, with an idea which had just occurred and which he presented in the same tone without aiming to make personal progress. 'Anyone as beautiful as you are, would have to appreciate the way they live, or nothing makes sense.'

She whipped round as if jabbed in the tabard by a dirk; but whatever she was going to say, was edited out when she saw his face. He was presenting a simple fact, like extra data to be

64

punched into a computer. There was nothing that rated an objection.

The delay gave time for the words to settle in. Even a top grade logistics expert is not chilled steel right through. She said, 'You really are concerned about them.'

'I've never seen a way of life which seemed more stable and satisfying for the average man.'

'The noble savage?'

'They're not savages. I suspect they've been where we are now. Farther on even. They've given it up. Settled for small groups with simple objectives.'

'Nobody can do that. Societies go forward or backward. There's no standing still.'

'What is progress? The first man who chipped out a hand axe and buried it in his neighbour's head was only doing what a disintegrator can do. Difference in quantity. No difference in kind. Cooking a meal over a fire is no different from thumbing down on a button a protein simulator. You're no better off.'

'The simulator frees you for something else.'

'Such as what?'

It was a good question and she was ready with a good answer; but they had arrived at journey's end in Sector B, a large office above the lock, and Hadden was watching them in with some suspicion. Clearly, he thought that Kirby was trying to subvert a loyal witness.

He said, 'Over here, Commander, next to me. Naturally I expected this development and I have been thinking about it. I have a blue-print for action for the next twenty-four hours. It is obviously vital that we strike at once.'

Kirby said, 'I am not, repeat not, taking *Cossack* into an attack on any ground installation until I know more about the attitude of the people.'

Hadden sat very still. He had expected a showdown in time; but it was to have been of his own choosing, when Kirby was

65

expendable. He said, 'Your attitude is well-known. I shall not forget this. You understand that I can put you under arrest and send *Cossack* under another officer?'

Kirby flipped a switch on his chest console and very faintly Tom Mowatt's voice joined the meeting in a brief announcement, 'Co-Pilot.'

'Captain. Bring *Cossack* round to the lock in B Sector. I shall be leaving in a few minutes.'

'*Cossack* to B Sector lock. Check.'

Kirby said, 'What action you might take when the squadron is on this station is one thing. The action you will take as of now is another. I'll tell you what I propose to do. I'll take *Europa* and a volunteer crew and go down to the settlement which was investigated by the first expedition. *Cossack* will stay on station and protect the convoy. If Martinez was right, there should be no problem. I can find out what agency is jamming the computers. Maybe they want more reassurances. A piece of paper with signatures on it. I'm sure Governor Maynard will satisfy them in that respect. If I am not back in twenty-four hours, you will have to carry on in whatever way you decide.'

Rosencrat paid his way as a member by saying, 'Surely that is an unnecessary risk. We cannot afford to lose *Europa*.' He added, too late for tact, 'or the trained personnel involved. Every ship will be needed to ferry down the labour force.'

Hadden was suddenly agreeable. He had seen it as a compromise which was not all bad. The few hours delay would not affect schedules in any substantial way. If it succeeded, his committee would have worked a neat diplomatic success and if it failed, Kirby was out of their hair. *Cossack* would be still available as a striking force and her crew nicely motivated with a grievance.

He said, 'Very well, Commander. I'll go along with that. You see we are all just as keen as you yourself to make this mission succeed in peace.'

Rosencrat said, 'That's very fair. Very fair indeed. You couldn't get anything fairer than that. I'll get a piece out about it. Everybody will like a fair deal like that.'

Unexpectedly, Barbara Hulse made a condition, she said, 'I'll agree to that, if I can be one of the party. I want to use my own judgement first hand.'

Hadden looked directly at Kirby, as though hoping to see proof of pre-knowledge. But surprise there was unaffected and obvious. Still, it started up a train of thought. Kirby's goose would be well-cooked, when the main party checked in and his scarcity value zeroed. But there was no harm in pushing a good thing along. A word in Maynard's ear that the military man was interested in Barbara Hulse would keep things moving.

Maynard's admin machine was efficient, whatever else. Forty minutes before first light, personnel changes were complete and Kirby was buckled in at the command console of *Europa*.

Here, he could feel that he was accepted. Without going into the details of the argument, the crew of *Europa* were inclined to support a professional in their own business against the administrators on *New World*.

Voices on the net, reminded him that he had a mixed crew. Renshaw, the commander, had taken top navigation slot, with a silvery-voiced girl, Janet Blair, as his second and Railton from *Cossack* at the third desk. Power was an all-male team, with Scholes in at Number three. Communications had a girl at number two whose voice virtually stopped the action, whenever she was moved to speech. It poured down the intercom like so much clotted cream and Kirby had the impression that much of it would clog every micro-relay on the board.

He got her name from the crew list and said, 'Greta.'

'Yes Commander,'—a minimum reply but it took time to filter through and carried with it a total willingness to oblige.

'Once we get under way, leave the chat to your exec. Working it out as we go, there just isn't time.'

'Certainly. Anything you say, Commander. And I don't mind a bit. I expect you're used to laconic, military precision and that. When I can't bear it another *second* I'll talk to the passenger.'

Barbara Hulse had been put in at Communications Three, a sinecure for a short trip, with mathematics involved that she could do in her head. She was listening to Greta Scott in amazement. In the higher echelons of professionalism, it was unusual to find straight *seraglio*.

It was strange, anyway, to be where she was. As a member of the inner circle of the Lasmec empire, she had been given real power from an early age. Communication Three was lowest berth in the ten man team running *Europa*.

Then there was enough to do to keep her mind off every other issue.

Kirby gently disengaged *Europa* without disturbing the transport's orbital path and backed away for a clear run. Without the computers, he was taking it on personal judgement. Habit made him call the shots as he made flight corrections. Normally, they would have been taken up, checked and fed back as precisely accurate instructions for the auto pilot.

This time there was silence. *Europa* began to dive in a long spiral which would take her in narrowing sweeps to a landing below the parked convoy.

Barbara Hulse spoke directly to her fellow mute at the communications desk. 'The math of this is all wrong. We'll end up in the sea.'

'Tell the man, dear. He'll just love that.'

Greta flicked through to the general net. Still loading every word with promise, she managed to get a fair turn of speed on to, 'Commander, the passenger has something *important* to tell you.'

Kirby said, 'All right, Number Three, let's have it.'

The answer was quick and explicit. Triopus coming up as though in a zoom lens made its own argument for speed.

He said, 'You could be right. I'll use your figures. Either way I would have to take the last leg as an atmosphere craft, by visual navigation. Stay with it then. Check me as I go.'

There followed a twenty minute chore which tasked her to the limit of her intellect's span. Breaking down the problems and farming them out to Greta Scott and Pearce the Number One, she managed to have answers ready to feed back, beating critical time lines by fractions of a second.

It was completely absorbing and she got an insight into how his mind worked, so that towards the end she was anticipating his next move.

When *Europa* was flexing down on her jacks within a hundred metres of the reference on his chart, he was sorry that the bond was broken. He said, 'Thank you, Dr Hulse. Your help was invaluable. Anything within a hundred kilometres would have been satisfactory. I was expecting to have to make an overland hop.'

Greta Scott, already tipping back her visor and heaving at the stud seals of her suit, said absently, 'You *are* clever, dear.' She was mainly concerned to fish out a cosmetic case cunningly built into the left shoulder of her corrugated shell. Then she was momentarily incommunicado, while she checked that all was well.

In an opposed idiom to the blonde Barbara, it was very well. High-piled black hair, very fine and with a built in luminous glow; high cheek bones; moulded, smooth, sleek look; prominent lips, full and pouting; small, round chin; large, heavy-lidded Epstein eyes. In profile, not out of place in a Minoan mural.

Kirby thought, not for the first time, that it was a minor miracle that the civilian ships survived any mission. There was a greater than even chance that outside was hostile and *Europa* ought to be ready to claw a way out of it at a second's notice.

With the crew getting set for a picnic on the grass, they would never make it.

Railton, Scholes and himself were the only ones still sealed up and ready for an operational roll. He said, and the external tannoy made no softening of the tone, 'Hold fast. Stay in your couches. Seal up.'

Greta said, 'I'm glad I'm not in the navy,' but she stopped her unnecessary repair work and was in fact first back to base. On the net she said, 'Here I am, Commander, all prone again. Do what you will.'

Kirby sent up the cone aerial probe, a thin tongue of high tensile steel, taking the viewing eye of the scanner a further fifty metres from the steeple. *Europa* stood a hundred and ninety metres on her tripod jacks. With the addition, the horizon was rolled back seventy kilometres.

Renshaw said, 'It looks peaceful enough.'

He was stating no more than the simple truth. Top right, Pearce had made an inset to show in miniature a full circle of territory in range. It was like a circular page-illustration in an atlas. Low hills, a winding river, wooden slopes, fields laid out in a regular patchwork of colour under cultivation for the half dozen staples used in food preparation. Grid lines of the canal system for irrigation and transport.

Blown up to show paving-stone detail, the rest of the screen carried a shot of the centre of the nearest township— visible anyway, end-on, from the direct vision port at their back.

Nothing moved. There was no traffic on the canal which bisected the town square. Of three house doors in view, two were closed, one was wide open to a shadowed interior.

It was a backdrop for a musical. Jolly villagers to enter left. Line of serving wenches with a bold one to say, 'Where be squire? I got a thing to say to he.'

Greta Scott who was type cast for it, in all but pace said, 'Where is everybody?'

It was a fair question. Kirby looked at the time disk. 0948 hours. He remembered mornings on Triopus. They were early starters, running their day firmly within the boundaries of natural light.

He said, 'Captain Renshaw. Be ready to take her up. I'll run out your freight car and check around. Scholes with me.'

Barbara Hulse said quickly, 'I should like to join you.'

His hesitation was fractional. First thought was that it might be dangerous for her, but it was followed by the judgement that if there was danger it would come to her anyway sooner or later. In the short term, it might be useful to have a witness who was firmly in the governor's councils and could not be accused of bias.

'Very well. Allow us one hour. If we are not back, your count down starts at 1050. Okay?'

Renshaw said, 'Ten fifty. Check.'

In the loading bay Kirby said, 'The air is good. Outside temperature is twenty-three. Leave suits here. They may be needed in a hurry.'

The last bit was to Barbara Hulse. Scholes was already setting his on a rack with the front panel peeled back like an anatomical model.

She said, 'I'm not dressed for an official reception.'

Scholes said gallantly, 'You'd be guaranteed a welcome on any inhabited planet in the galaxy.'

Out of the corrugated shell, she stood revealed in a pale sapphire leotard. Little more than a pastel-shaded nude. Drifted to any shore she would be an obvious ambassadress of peaceful intentions.

Kirby suddenly began to feel optimistic. In spite of the massive organization behind the colonization bid, it had worked round to this. He was back in person and first ashore. Surely there was a pattern in it somewhere?

They stood on the metre square platform of the loading trolley and the freight elevator took them down. Heat was still rising from the scorched ground and radiating from the ship's cooling skin.

A gauge on the pedestal console hit thirty before Kirby could move them off. Half tracks bit into the burnt earth and they ran out of hot reeking shadow into sunlight and meadow-scented air.

Hoops front and rear made anchor points for standing passengers. Kirby, feet astride hung on to grabs on the console and pushed up the speed until they were making half a kilometre a minute over a long, level pasture of blue-green grass.

Close to the ground, it seemed incredibly, dangerously fast. But exhilarating, in a way that the fantastic speeds of space flight were not. Barbara Hulse's hair was flying straight back like a shining pennant to match the small blue and white Western Hemisphere emblem straining at a whippy, aerial mast.

Speed fell away, and they were bucking a short hummocky rise to meet a paved strip running beside a canal. Two minutes later, they were circling the square of the settlement with still no sign of jolly welcoming villagers or indeed villagers of any kind.

Barbara Hulse said, 'Is this where you landed before?'

'Yes. Over the other side.'

Kirby went off along the canal until they were out of the village. Half a kilometre and he ran off through a broad border of low shrubs until they came out on more open pasture. Dead ahead was a huge circle of sparse growth with bare, blackened patches where grass had not yet grown.

They looked at it in silence. *Europa Nine*'s searing rockets had left a mute, but indelible testament.

Scholes said, 'That's a ship's mark sure enough. What do you think happened to the people, skipper?'

'Let's take a closer look.'

Going into the houses, Kirby remembered the custom that no door was ever locked, even at night. They started at the first house, by itself, surrounded by a trim garden. Wall sconces were fitted with fresh torches, the floor swept clean. It had the look of a chalet prepared for hire.

Barbara Hulse went through into a low-ceilinged bedroom,

white-walled, scented; windows open to a long view of distant hills. She called back, 'Either this bed has not been slept in or someone was up early to tidy the room.'

In the kitchen, there was food in storage bins. Loaves of honey-coloured bread, jars of paste made from nut kernels, long purple vegetable roots. No evidence that a meal had been recently prepared or eaten. Fuel set ready in a cold brazier.

In spite of the light and the sense of small-scale domestic peace, the total absence of a recognizable human agent made its mark. Barbara shivered suddenly. She went to the window and stood looking out.

Kirby's eyes from the doorway brought her round and he saw that her eyes were troubled.

Her mood communicated to him.

'Uncanny, isn't it?'

She said, 'I have an odd feeling that I've been here before.'

'I don't know any landscape on Earth planet that could remind you of it.'

'It's not that. Not the view anyway. The room itself and . . .'

'Yes?'

But she did not go on. It was something to do with him. She had been aware of him moving about in the outer room and had expected him to be standing there by the door in white coveralls. There was a difference though. In her mind's eye, she had seen him swaying on his feet, with a long tear down his left side and blood welling in a spreading stain.

She was very quiet as they went on with the search. Everywhere it was the same. After the first six, Kirby took every third and then every tenth. They were in the elevator going up into *Europa* with a minute to go for the deadline.

Kirby said flatly, 'There's no problem. This site is deserted. Maynard can get his riggers down and build his reception camp.'

Chapter Five

Dawn came up on Triopus with long flushes of cadmium yellow, patches of rose madder in full hue and thin, etiolated bars of viridian.

Grant Kirby watched it in the control cabin of *Cossack*, the fifteenth such, since the official founding of the city. *Europa* and *Philadelphia* rose like huge triangulation points left and right. Neatly centred from the three ships, was the growing spread of workshops and dormitory blocks. Temporary power lines criss-crossed the site. Light spilled coldly from every window.

Some optimist, with Eldorado in mind, had painted 'Dawson City' on the roof of the admin centre. Certainly, compared with the empty township, it had a raw, last frontier look.

Barbara Hulse saw it across a garden and a canal from the window of a cottage. As there was no vertical division of accommodation by rank, top A-category personnel had been given horizontal demarkation in a residential canton patrolled by security guards with a house each.

She watched the distant hills pass the colour threshold and show up in a cover of green foliage. Overhead *New World* was a bright asterisk of silver. Beyond it two moons were spaced out in equidistance.

For as long as she could remember, she had been deeply involved in an important project. There had hardly been time for introspection or any search for herself as a person.

Living to some extent alone for the last weeks, she had looked inside more than ever before and had begun to question where she was and where she was going.

Life at the top with Maynard would be no problem. She

74

was well adjusted to it. The kind of future all her acquaintances had accepted as a standard. Now she doubted whether it was enough.

There was no escape from it in any event. A contract was a contract, the very fabric of the social pattern.

Looking at the moons again, she was struck by their symmetry. They appeared as identical featureless disks. She remembered them in their setting with the other two. A perfect tetrahedron. That surely was unusual in the random conditions of creation. Odds against it must be fantastic.

Her mathematician's mind began to work on it.

Still thinking about it, she went through into the kitchen. From that window she could see the embryo reception area and the towering corvette.

Kirby would be interested about the moons. It was surprising that he hadn't noticed it. Perhaps he had, anyway. Since they settled in she had not seen him. *Cossack* was on a continuous round of watchdog missions. Twice a day up to the satellite, two or three patrol orbits round Triopus, then down again.

He was doing a good job. She felt guilty about him, knowing that Maynard and Hadden were set on discarding him as soon as it was safe so to do.

She looked at her time disk—a complex miniature set in a filigree scarab, Maynard's formal contract gift. 0730 hours. Half an hour yet before she was due at her desk. Time to walk over to *Cossack* and talk to Kirby about the moons.

She spent three minutes—which was a thirty-three percent increase on normal—fixing her hair in a white headband and set off along the blue canal to work round to the launch pad.

Half way there and the ground began to vibrate. *Cossack* was suddenly shrouded in a curtain of white vapour. She stood still and watched its slow lift develop into a surge and an orange fireball elongate into a soaring flame.

She felt, unreasonably, that it was a personal affront. A rejection. Work is the great therapy. Early at her desk, she began to check through a flow problem which had come up on the night detail.

Cossack nosed into a docking collar on the satellite. Sibley and Parkes were outside within the minute and drumming a call on Sector A lock. It opened up on a count of ten. The residents were improving all the time.

Fifty riggers with two foremen were still manning the hulk. After the crowded days of the passage they felt the isolation and were glad of the physical link with the shore.

Already the shell was substantially changed. Many interior divisions had been dismantled and sent down for planned use in ground installations. Destined as the centre hub of a permanent space station, the core had been cleared to a vast echoing cavern. Eventually it would be able to accept a freighter in its belly for mechanical discharge of cargo into storage bays.

Grant Kirby filled in time with Mowat at the main scanner. He was still looking for signs of life on Triopus.

Time and again, they pinpointed a likely spot for a settlement and blew the picture up until even the grass was discrete and identifiable as a separate plant.

Mowat said, 'It's a big place. Unless you had a map reference you could spend a lifetime in random selection and see nothing.'

'If we don't find an answer we might not have a lifetime.'

'How long before the main force shows up?'

'May be a month.'

'They'll need briefing on local conditions. Ninety cans milling about without exact course data won't be good.'

'You can signal that in another week.'

'Not unless this interference clears up. It's jamming on 1490.'

'We have a little time. If there's no other way, we can take a day's run out and RV.'

'What can they do in a day?'

'What can they do in a month? There's no turning back and no other planet they can reach.'

Kirby crossed to a direct vision port and watched Sibley and Parkes moving deliberately out of Sector A lock. Mowat's voice cut across his thought that their patient work was very like whistling in the dark.

'Something here, Grant.'

It was the open square of a settlement, identical to the one at the reception area. Except in one important particular. A dark slim girl wearing a red kaftan and high-heeled sandals, walking with short steps, so that she seemed to glide, was crossing an open space between two houses.

Mowat keyed in the reference and a tiny speck of yellow light glowed on the inset map. Reading off the grid, he said, 'Eleven hundred kilometres from Dawson City. There's got to be something nearer than that.'

'Could be. But this one is sure. We can reach it overland in a scout car in half a day.'

'Maynard won't want to know. He's happy to go ahead without meeting a resident.'

'Maynard will still have to do it the way I say.'

'Have you thought about that, Grant? He's not one to take opposition on the long term. Every day that passes without outside interference makes *Cossack* that much less important.'

'I know that. He can't move until he gets a replacement. And the squadron will see it as I do.'

'Some might. Some won't. Wilkes has a following right through the corps. There are political men. What about Greyson?'

Greyson of *Gurkha* had been appointed straight to a command slot from outside the service against Halsall's opinion. It was said he was a plant by a syndicate with armament interests.

'Well it's my problem. Get Sibley in and cast off. One orbit and down to base. Then break out the scout car. We'll make that settlement before dark.'

Kirby, although not intending to take any answer but yes, went through the proper channels to set up his safari. He spoke to Hadden from the pad with *Cossack* wreathed in clouds of grey coolant.

Hadden said, 'You will leave *Cossack* operational, of course. I suggest that you take only one crewman with you. Naturally I shall ask the Governor to send along a representative. Give me fifteen minutes and I will call you.'

'If it is longer than fifteen minutes, I shall have gone.'

Hadden's face faded quickly from the scanner. Not so fast however that his tight-lipped acceptance of the deadline did not register.

Mowat said, 'Laughing boy needs watching.'

Whatever his feelings, the Defence Minister had moved fast. Seven minutes later his face was in again. 'There will be two civilian members of your party. Dr Hulse will represent the Governor. She has asked for another woman from *Europa* to accompany her as a companion. You will pick them up at my office.' He did not add that the invitation was his own idea and that he proposed to tell Maynard about it when the party had left. A small thing which might or might not pay off. But every planet should have its Iago.

With Scholes at the console, *Cossack*'s small scout car threaded a way through the crowded site and dropped on its skids under a half-built entrance porch. Two trim figures in white zipper suits with calf length boots were already there present. The taller, fair one had a sling pack of standard recording gear on one shoulder. Her vividly dark companion had her pack behind her, with its narrow strap neatly deployed down the centre of her chest adding tension to its already generous contour. This one opened the conversation in strict *legato* with, 'You should be very flattered, Commander, to find us all ready and waiting for you.'

The scout car circled the camp once, climbing to a ceiling of fifty metres. Scholes picked up the bearing and went over to auto pilot at a steady 150 kilometres in the hour and virtually disappeared from sight. Micro grooving on its hull gave it an iridescent shimmer which was camouflage against ground or sky. Its four occupants were in a small, lost, hurrying world of their own.

Inside its compact hull, however, there was enough human pressure to make existence plain enough. Exotic scent from Greta Scott imported a domestic note from the start. It was a full time chore to keep the mission on a military footing.

Two hours and three hundred kilometres on, Bob Scholes had already hauled down his flag, and Greta was saying, 'Surely, Grant, its time for a picnic on the grass?'

They had crossed forest and plain; two, slow-moving rivers; an inland lake that might rank as a sea, blue and tranquil; two settlements, identical with the one at base and equally deserted. Now Scholes switched out the robot and planed down to a precise landing in the shade of a copse of seven towering sequoia with spade leaves like scarlet shovels.

He whipped out in the best traditions of service to be at hand to lift out Greta's ration pack.

Kirby, slower off the mark was at hand to meet the queen bee, but whether by accident or design she beat him to it and was out moving well before he could throw down his cloak.

He followed up with a standard meal pack from the locker. Self heating minestrone, savoury protein block, fruit bar and coffee.

Under the shade of the huge trees even Greta went quiet, but it was a companionable silence.

When they had finished Scholes stood up, brushed crumbs off his chest and then grabbed Greta's wrist. 'Five minutes walk, fatso, before you get it parked for another long sit. Is that okay, Skipper?'

'That's okay. Stay in sight of the car.'

'I'm the one who should be asked.' It was a statement of despair. She was already hauled to her feet and likely to be dragged like a lissom log if she didn't begin to walk.

As they went out of sound range, she was saying, 'Lying down *flat* is just as much a change from sitting, as standing up *straight*. You have no imagination, Bob.'

'Too much imagination is what I've definitely got. Come on now, big breaths and step it out.'

Back at the laager there was a silence which lengthened into a negative statement that there was something between them to watch out for.

He had a covering occupation in collecting the few stores they had used and returning them to the locker. She remembered her early morning bid to speak to him about the moon formation. It sounded false to her own ears as she said it, but it got them off the ground into a reasonable piece of dialogue

'There was something this morning I wanted to ask you about, but when I started off for *Cossack* it was too late. You went off on patrol.'

'What was that, then?'

'The moons. The four moons of Triopus.'

'It's not unusual. Some inhabited planets have a dozen or more. Makes for complex tides. Weather patterns too, very unpredictable.'

It was all very well making conversation, but a patronizing hand-out like that was not on. She said, 'Yes, I'm well aware of that angle. But here the opposite seems to be true.'

'The opposite?'

'Regularity. You saw them as we came in. Well, I suppose you see them every day. They make a regular tetrahedron. And as far as I can judge they seem to be the same size. If it wasn't impossible, you could say that it was man-made.'

Kirby clipped down the locker lid and weighed his reply. He even turned round to deliver it. She was sitting on her heels, knees out at a ninety degree angle looking up at him.

What he was going to say took a second check. Something about the pose she was in, tautly controlled vigour of thighs and throat angled back, presented her more completely as a sexual object than any yet, flame shift included. A line came into his mind, '*Ces grappes de ma vigne*'. But he did not stop to ravel back the association to its hole.

The delay made its mark and intuition gave her some at least of the background signal. She stood up, brushing bits of blue grass from her pants, not looking at him.

Kirby released to speech said, 'It's true I haven't ever seen a formation so exact. But with an infinity of possible combinations, pure chance would throw up one or two.'

'That's so; but it puts a big restriction on the field when you consider only inhabited planets.'

'It's something we ought to look at certainly. Tomorrow or the next day, I'll fit a moon drop into the patrol schedule. Take one a day and check them out.'

'I'd like to go along.'

'That could be arranged. We carry some general duties personnel. You could double at one of the computer stations.'

When it was out and said, hanging about in the warm air like a genie out of a bottle, he recognized that he had broken a long term rule about civilians on board his ship.

Scholes appeared, rounding the bole of a sequoia still leading Greta by the hand like figures on an antique vase.

Greta said, 'He's a *monster*. Do you know he hasn't stopped *once*.'

Kirby took the pilot seat and pushed them on for another two-hour stint. Below them the relief map rolled out. A small-scale intimate landscape with no grandeurs and no trash heaps. For over a hundred kilometres, they flew five metres above the uniform ceiling of a continuous forest. Regular as a plantation.

Scholes said, 'What do you make of the timber, Skipper?'

'Planned growth by all appearance, but I wouldn't know why.'

Greta, to show that she was a well-informed girl, said, 'It could be for climate control. Forestation makes a big difference.'

'There's at least one other odd feature about it.' Barbara Hulse lifted her head from a viewer which gave back seat passengers an interest. Geared to collect and trap still frames at any given rate, it could be used in conjunction with recording equipment to take map samples for an area. She had been watching ten flashes a minute over a period and came up with a mathematician's gloss. 'It's a ninety-nine-point-nine-nine probability that there's no wild life of any kind in this wood. No birds even.'

Kirby said, 'That figures. The people we investigated before were vegetarians. There were no domesticated animals either.'

The climatology expert had not shot her last intellectual bolt, she said. 'However do they get on without the birds and the bees? I thought that old fertility cycle would grind to a halt if they stopped working their tiny fingers to the bone.'

Scholes slewed round in his seat and was all admiration.

'What are you looking at, you big ape?'

'It is interesting to see someone with such a one-track mind. A dedicated type you might say.'

Greta appealed to the driver. 'Grant, I think your soldier is being rude to me. Will you put the back seat off limits. Except for senior ranks, of course. You're welcome.'

Barbara Hulse, following the conversation with minimal attention, found the last bit meaningful. She looked at Kirby to see how he was reacting. That would be a real possibility. How did she feel about that?

It ought not to concern her. Once the contract with Maynard was ratified she was bound for a minimum period of five years.

Even after that, renewal of contract was automatic unless there were strong incompatibility grounds. That was something again. Hardly anybody could build a case without looking a fool. During the first five-year stint, adjustment clinics were available to do a brain-washing job until the two sides were on common ground on every social attitude. Compulsorarily so. The state could not afford instability at the family level.

It was a train of thought which led her to Maynard. Was she prepared to be tailored to fit into his personality pattern? Or was it that she thought they were so close that no adjustment would be needed?

Once the questions were raised she had to find honest answers. They were two hundred kilometres further on when she decided that the answers were definitely not affirmative. It took another fifty to bring her round to the view that in the absence of a middle category, she had to say 'no'.

Simultaneously, in another part of the planet, Maynard was doubting the wisdom of letting her in on the top level executive floor before he had the legal right to check out her attitudes. As a Lasmec, inner wheel, there ought to have been no doubt; but over the last weeks he had been surprised by her out-of-line opinions on a number of issues.

Too sure of his own many-sided excellence for self-doubt, he could not see any girl—even one from the Lasmec stable—being anything but delighted by chance of a contract. Hadden's bit of politic poison went largely wasted.

But he was not pleased to find that she was off on a trip that might take anything up to twenty hours.

Even the aim of it was suspect. He said, 'I'm surprised you sanctioned it. What good can it do? We know there's no problem from local opposition. In six months, we'll have the colony so well-established that nothing can challenge it. Kirby's at it again. Going out of his way to find somebody to put up an objection.'

Hadden said, 'He's definitely shown himself against the project all along the line. It makes a real case for taking him out of any position of power. In the public interest.'

'I know that. We can't move against him until the rest of the military force shows up. His crew is loyal to him. We've been into all that.'

'At the moment he doesn't have his crew. If anything happened to him on this trip, Mowat could take over. He'd be an efficient commander and wouldn't ask as many questions.'

Maynard riffled through a stack of punched card reports. He wanted to get on with playing them on his pianola. Not for the first time, he thought that the advantages of having a devious subordinate could be outweighed by not knowing what he was on about.

'That's all very well. You allowed Dr Hulse to go with him. She couldn't be got out of the way without showing your hand.'

'I'll think about it.'

'Do that. Don't let me know what you decide. I'm fully committed here.'

It was conditional agreement and Hadden was satisfied. He left the Governor feeding a card into his helpmeet's ear and went next door to his own office.

The psychology of the individual was the big gag here. He reckoned he could bank on Kirby's reaction to a power failure in the scout car. Make it just far enough out to be a hard forced-march back to base. With a radio blanket on for ground transmissions outside a few kilometres range there would be no sitting tight and sending out a signal for help. Ten to one Kirby would leave the two women in the shuttle and set out with Scholes to bring up a relief car. Peaceful, empty countryside. They couldn't come to any harm.

No need even for a direct confrontation. Pick them up on a well hidden scanner. A laser beam from cover. Clean quick job with everybody happy.

Hadden looked at himself with some satisfaction in the dark blank of his inter-office video. He bared his teeth and stroked his moustache with the tip of his right index finger—a self-congratulatory gesture he was much given to.

'You're very clever,' he told himself. 'A very clever, far-sighted bastard. You'll do well here. I shouldn't be surprised if you don't get to be very important in this place. Top man even and have blondie all to yourself, if that's what you want.'

Ever prudent, even in reflective train, he looked again at that statement of aim and found it reasonable. Without being emotionally concerned, she would do very well. Set the seal on his progress in the Lasmec organization.

In about one hour they would reach journey's end. Say one hour on the site. That would be long enough to chat up a few natives if they found any. Minimum six hours back. Plenty of time. Stop them about a hundred kilometres out? That would be a nice distance for Kirby's gallant, homeward slog. Any records they had in the car too could be quietly disappeared. Barbara Hulse could be persuaded to say nothing for the public good and the other girl hardly knew what time of day it was.

A nice refinement that. He checked a flow diagram on his office wall and found a work party index number, then he thumbed down a call stud. A young face came up, wearing a construction-worker's white helmet, eager to oblige.

'Yes, Controller Hadden?'

'Very prompt, Sanders. Glad to see you're on your toes down there. Get me foreman Lomax and have him come up here right away.'

Darkness on Triopus was never absolute. Starlight alone would make it impossible. Four moons sharing the chore added a pale shadowless flood only marginally below the colour threshold.

Even the hurrying car cast no shadow. It passed like a faint gleam, a flicker of iridescence.

After twelve hours together, its human freight had stopped making conversation. Greta, in the rumble, with its squab angled back, had twisted lithely in her straps, settled her dark head on Scholes' shoulder and was comfortably asleep. In the green, hooded light from the console her skin looked startlingly white like chiselled marble. Heavy as stone at that after a time. But Scholes was careful not to disturb her.

He said in a whisper, 'How long to go, Skipper?'

The vibration in his chest echoed in her ear and she said in tones even more relaxed and velvety than normal, 'That reminds me about that man with a fishbone in his throat who made an urgent visit to a doctor's consulting room on his precinct.'

Scholes, taken by surprise, gave her the feed line, 'What happened to him, then?'

'Well, this very pretty nurse opened the door and he said in a hoarse whisper, "Is the doctor about?" '

Greta sat up to get the rest of it right. She was also giggling too much to get it out.

Scholes flexed his stiff arm, thinking that it was an ill wind that blew nobody any good.

Greta drew a deep breath which even in the green gloom was an impressive sight. She said, 'This bit always kills me. This nurse *whispered* back, "No. Come in".'

Still delighted, she went back to her nest with unerring aim as though she had never left it.

After this late, late show, Scholes tried again. 'How much farther?'

'Less than an hour.'

'Can I take her in?'

'No stay where you are. You're doing a good public relations job there.'

'It's a pleasure.'

The break in silence did something to ease Kirby's mood. He looked at Barbara. Lit from below by the green light her face was strange and hardly recognizable. Smiling, however, she certainly was. Teeth very white in the hard light.

He said, 'A fool's errand. Wasted your valuable time. Not that I understand it. People were there for a sure thing.'

There was some bitterness in his voice and she had an illuminating insight into what he must be feeling. It would not be easy for him to report to Hadden and ultimately to Maynard that he had been wrong again. Or if not wrong, unable to bring any evidence back.

It had not taken long to establish that the township was as empty as if nobody had ever lived there. A folk museum in good repair, like the one at base. They had run in at dusk, with lengthening shadows. Not a sound, not a light. But a feeling that she remembered from childhood, common to that time of day. Expectancy, as though they were on the verge of a great revelation, as though something could happen which would change all future time for them.

Whatever it was, carried conviction. Suddenly they had felt threatened by the spirit of the place. Out on a limb with no defence, surrounded by a wasteland. She had been glad when Kirby had cut short the search and said shortly, 'Okay. Back to base.'

Now she said as though her own opinion had clarified out, knowing that it would help him, 'If anything, not finding them is more serious than finding them hostile. It means they knew we were going to that particular place at that time. How did they know? Where did they go? *How* did they go, if it comes to that?'

The same question marks were set up in permanent display round the periphery of his own mind. He was spared a confession of ignorance by developments external to them both. Like Scholes, he could claim that it was an ill wind.

After so many hours, the thin high whine of the scout car's

power pack had passed into a background noise which was no longer heard. Surf to those living by the sea. Now, it dropped down the tonal scale a full octave, held G in alt for a half second and cut right out.

Split second reaction times moved Grant Kirby to the miniature console before the hum had died away.

Instant diagnosis led him to expect a fault in the auto-pilot. When there was no joy on manual, he knew nothing he could do would stop a crash landing.

They were out of the forest area, passing to the right of an empty settlement. Fields, hedgerows, a canal. Deceleration was pinning him back with a $\frac{1}{2}$G thrust. He crossed a hedge with centimetres under the skids, fighting to keep the car's nose from turning down.

When they hit, he thought he had done it. Skids tore free and the silver bullet ploughed through grass and loam on its underbelly; then a transverse drainage ditch crossed their path and the car spent its last units of garnered kinetic urge in rolling base over tip to end flat on its back.

From the time the motor ceased to deliver to the time when they hung upside down from their straps with a rain of small trash falling round them, could be counted in seconds. As sudden a reversal of fortune as any tragedy-writing computer could feed on the primary plot line.

Greta Scott found herself in a bear hug giving more comprehensive comfort than any harness. Looked at from the underside, where any silver lining was bound to show, the situation was not all bad. She said, 'This is a curious position for a girl to find herself in,' and then proved that isometric drills paid off, by taking her weight and some of his on her toes while Scholes busied himself with release studs.

Light still glowed from the console panel and Grant Kirby talked soothingly to his passenger. The only one not trained to accept the vagaries of flight as good clean fun, she was less sure that all manner of things would be well.

Her rope of yellow hair hung straight down to an S-coil on the roof. Her eyes were dilated wide and she was holding on to the grabs on the floor beside the seat in silent and inward-looking despair.

He saw she was safe enough for the moment and freed himself. Then he knelt immediately below her, chocking her left shoulder with his right to take her weight when the straps came loose.

Against the side of his face, through thin, taut fabric, he could feel her heart pounding like an independent machine in a warm, pneumatic sheath.

When the harness came free there was hardly any increase in weight and he had to talk to her to break her convulsive grip on the sky bolts. Quietly, as though to a child. As though they were alone. In fact, the physical contact had put everything else out of mind. Triopus, the mission, his danger, everything had gone except the immediate closed circuit intimacy of her particular scent and particular stimuli to sense.

He said, 'Rapunzel, Rapunzel, open your hands,' in the tones of a fairy-tale teller.

Anything authoritative would have made her cling more tightly. She was in a strange limbo and being upside down was a top-line symbol for it. For the first time in her life she was uncertain about herself and about people. Add to that a constitutional fear about falling from a height and the current set-up had her in a unique state of being sensitive.

His voice and its semi-humorous gloss on the childhood tale hit the right frequency for obedience and she let go her grip, leaving it to the man to sort it all out.

It was not done without some refined balancing and controlled brute force. One part of her mind registered surprise that he should have such reserves of sheer strength.

When she was kneeling, chest to chest with him on the deck, he did not at once release his grip. They were breathing together in the same rhythm. Aware of each other. Eyes threaded on a double string for the half minute that their minds grappled with a communication problem on their own level, reluctant to admit that the pass had been sold elsewhere.

Greta's voice in belated concern, 'Are you all right, Barbara?' sounded forced as indeed it was. 'Hold it, Bob. Just a *minute*.'

Kirby let her go. With the physical break, his own problems flooded in. As of now, there was the major one of getting his party back.

When Barbara Hulse answered for herself, he felt the warmth of her breath. Who was it who had said the three qualities to seek in a woman were sweet breath, firm breasts and a flat diaphragm? That put it on the top line on all counts. But it was a cynic's dictum. She would be top line, for him in ways that could not be defined on a schedule.

Outside, they were in a paste-board world of black and white silhouettes. The car's undercarriage was a twisted wreck. Two forward lifting vents were sheared off. Without major refit she would not move again.

With an outline scheme forming, he said, 'Put her back right way up. Push along this line.'

The car rolled easily and settled with a crunch of collapsing struts on a roughly even keel.

Kirby said, 'We don't have a choice. Without communication somebody has to go on foot. As I see it there's no threat from any local agents, so the two women stay here. Or in the village over there, and we make a forced march. The going couldn't be easier, open country, paths even, nice climate. We'll do it in two days. Then half an hour to come out in a shuttle. There's food for a week in the emergency packs. No problem, just a nuisance.'

'Hadden will send out a car when we're overdue.' Barbara spoke directly to him for the first time since he had set her free. He knew without her saying it that she had edited out 'Maynard' and substituted 'Hadden' by a form of instinctive tact.

But he took it at face value and said, 'Could be. But this car is not easy to see. They don't know the exact line we are on. A searching craft could pass five kilometres either side and miss us altogether. No. This is the sure way. If they come out it cuts short the time. If not, we don't waste any. What do you want to do? Look at the village over there or stay in the car?'

'Neither. We'll come with you.'

'No. You stay here.'

Outside intervention resolved it. Greta said, 'The car for my money. Better the devil you know. There's too much appearing and disappearing in those houses. I'm not madly keen even about a friendly spirit.'

Scholes' massive arm round her waist forced an amendment for she was basically an honest girl. 'Well, a friendly-spirit spirit.'

Before they left, Kirby talked to the expert. With the girls settled down on a seat each, and the atmosphere boost still delivering a comfortable warmth, they lifted off an external cowling and looked at the power pack.

'What went wrong, Bob?'

'I've been thinking about that ever since she stalled. Nothing like it that I know. These packs are good for a lifetime service. Besides, with most faults you'd get a build up. Notice to quit.'

'That's the way I see it.'

'What about these Triopus people? If they can interfere with computers and put out a radio blank, they could have a shut-down beam.'

'It's possible, but I don't think so. We'll take a look round here before we go on.'

Opening the hatch to the ladies rest room, Kirby put in his head to say goodbye. From Barbara, he got a steady, considering look and a voice, barely audible, saying simply, 'Good luck.'

Greta Scott had pulled a fine scarf from the neck of her

coveralls and was holding it across her face like a yashmak. She said, 'Take care of yourselves and remember, Trust in God, but tie your camel.'

Scholes said, 'Thank you, Yasmin.'

Two kilometres away, Lomax picked them up on his scanner and watched them move circumspectly towards the hamlet. A precise pattern of cover and movement. First Kirby and then Scholes dropping out of sight while the other one made a run. Leapfrogging forward until they went out of range into the first house.

It looked as though it would be a long, busy night.

Chapter Six

From the windows of the house, the wrecked car could not be seen. There was only the motionless backdrop of Triopus. Distant black rim of hills, long fields, pale glitter of a canal.

They could be anywhere they had yet seen, except in the forest. Every settlement had the same simple setting, even the apparently random scatter of houses was duplicated. As though one plan had been found to be exactly suited to the needs of the citizenry.

Scholes said, 'There'd be no big pull on a man to find out what was in the next valley, when he knew it was just like the one he was in. What stops them being bored into a stupor?'

'Places aren't dynamic in themselves. It's a question of attitude. People are more important on that tack than where you happen to be.'

Kirby was remembering Barbara Hulse and had to make a deliberate effort to get his mind on the mission. 'Look around, Bob. We might as well know if they left recently.'

'Could be a day, could be a week.' Scholes went through into the kitchen and lifted the polished wooden lid of an earthenware bread bin. In the small white circle of a hand torch, three loaves stood inside; long torpedoes, one shorter than other two. He pulled the short one out and called, 'Commander, something here.'

A good five centimetres had been broken roughly from the point. Kirby touched the inside, and stood very still. It was spongy, underbaked even. But it had not dried out, even on the surface.

'What do you think, Skipper?'

'Put that light out. Get to the window and see what you can see.'

Kirby made a circuit of the remaining rooms. There was no change outside in any direction. When he got back, he said, 'We checked every house at base. There was never one item disturbed or half-used. Somebody's been here and broken that bread. This whole thing begins to send up a smell.'

'Triopus people?'

'I'd say not.'

'Somebody doesn't like us.'

'That would have to be Hadden. It was very quickly set up. Not many will know what we were doing.'

'They wouldn't bring us down just to say "How". And the madame. They stuck their necks out there. Hadden wouldn't risk killing Maynard's girl.'

'Not much risk yet. God, they'd expect either you or me to be able to plane a car down on an open field. Nicely chosen distance too.'

Grant Kirby felt suddenly insulted that anyone could have estimated so exactly what he would do. Hadden must think he was a fool. Well, he was nearly right. How would they set it up? There could be a dozen ways of setting out from this settlement. With only a small force, and Hadden would use as few as possible, they would have to set up a monitor. Watch that careful ploy up to the house. Somebody laughing a big belly laugh beside a screen.

Here they were out of sight; but as soon as they went through the door, they would be picked up, if his judgement was correct. Whether it was correct or not, he had to act as if it was so.

He said, 'Where would you site a scanner to watch a car in that field?'

'First choice, right here. But with restricted range, somewhere out there in a gully.'

'Where would you aim to drop a homing pigeon?'

'You'd have to see him pass and then follow up. Unless he came right to where you were and who could guarantee that?'

'That's the way I see it. Just here, we're on extreme range—

given these conditions—for anything sited well for that field. A little smoke and we could get out without being seen at once. A small receptor on long range will take a lot of handling. Out the back, get into the canal and swim down a couple of hundred metres. Out by a drainage gully and work round.'

Lomax saw the first wreath of smoke go up with only minor irritation. He said, 'They've lit a fire in there. Bedding down for the night away from temptation.'

His ditch-mate, Stelfox, a long, sallow-faced man who could have slipped unnoticed into any Hogarth print said, 'Fryin' their flamin' selves more like.'

A tongue of flame licked up beside the window they were watching and a figure apparently beating at it with a cloth. Dark smoke billowed out through the door.

Lomax said, 'They'll have to come out. Keep a roving scan round the smoke. See where they go.'

Five minutes later, he knew that he had lost them.

Stelfox said, 'How'm I supposed to get a fix with this flamin' mush on. You've had it, boss, and that's a fact.'

'Keep trying or you'll have it and that's another fact.'

'I'll have to start from zero and circle out. It's the only sure way.'

'Come on. Come on. Start then.'

Stelfox's simple logic was proven to the last premise. He zeroed every dial, fed in full power and selected a ten-metre circuit for a first run.

The face that came up filled the screen so completely that it was hardly recognizable as human geography. There was some excuse for doubt. Kirby was wet from the canal, streakily carboned by his fire-raising, teeth bared in a grimace of effort to cover the last few metres before the balloon went up.

Lomax was rat-quick to sort out the angles. However it had been done, he knew he was fighting for his life. The operator was still looking open-mouthed at the self-zooming picture on his screen, when the foreman had grabbed up a two-handed, heavy-duty laser and was spraying over the ditch top.

Kirby threw himself flat as the nozzle chopped down towards him and a fine furrow opened up like a dark line racing towards him in the moonlight. He had gathered himself to roll left when the line stopped in a single spurt of dust.

Foreman Lomax toppled out of his gully neatly filleted down the spine as Scholes took his target set up in silhouette.

Now there was no picture on the screen to hold Stelfox mesmerized and he was plucking his own laser from a convenient clip beside the set when Grant Kirby, feeling light weight and recharged with energy now that the action had begun, bored a terminal hole through his head. Night blacker than any in space filled his eyes.

Scholes said, 'They'll have land lines out to the ambush parties. Small intercom videos taking this programme.'

'Surely.' Kirby was already checking out the back of the console. 'Here they go. Left and right. Two.'

Scholes said, 'Whatever they used to bring us down will be in their car. Take a whole lot of power.'

'You're right at that. So it's near. Now if they've seen that picture, they'll be falling back to investigate, so the sooner we find that car the better.'

Thirty metres down the gully, its walls had been cut back to make an oval pit with the car set in it like a stone in a bezel. Blue fishnet tufted with grass was stretched over the gap. From ten metres, it melded into the background and disappeared.

Once inside, Scholes activated a miniature, built-in scanner. He back tracked along the ditch and they saw the first searcher drop down to ask Lomax what it was all about. Getting no satisfaction, he signalled briefly back the way he had come and was joined by a second man.

Suddenly the delicacy of their own position seemed to dawn on them. They were climbing out to find living room in the open countryside, when Scholes brought the car sidling crabwise over the field and Kirby, standing by the open hatch, made a methodical job of execution.

It was a civilian car with no permanent gunnery potential but it had four searchlight beams which could be dropped like perpendicular columns.

Scholes followed a land line, its fine thread showing up like silver in the battery of light. They found its terminal in a border of bushes beside the road and the disenchanted assassins fifteen metres away, crawling in single file down a drainage ditch.

This time, Kirby had to drive himself. He recognized that it was a military situation and that he had been the elected victim, that men could be detailed to carry out a murder were no cosmic loss; but it was still against the grain. Edgy with self-contempt, he fairly snarled at Scholes, 'Down left. Down. Hold it. Steady as you go. Steady, I say.'

It was a relief when one of them began to shoot into the underbelly of the car and a ripsaw line carved up the floor.

When it was done, he said, 'Down, Bob. Load them with the winch.'

Over in the village, the burning cottage was a pillar of fire. He said, 'Collect them all and shove them in that house. Clean the place up.'

Taking two at a time, they made bombing runs over the heart of the flame and dropped them in from the freight hatch. As Kirby knelt to shove Lomax out he saw his own hands holding the body. Sensitive, brown, sinewy. Not long ago they had been holding Barbara Hulse. There was no sense or reason in it.

He was suddenly angry in a way that he had never been before in his life. He knew, also, that this time it would not pass. The murderer's role had been forced on him and he was sick to death of belonging to a social group which could angle a man into such a corner.

Scholes set the civilian car down beside the wreck and came

nearer to joining his ancestors than at any time yet this hard day's night.

He crossed to the scout car, drummed two-fisted on its hatch panel and shouted 'Bring out your dead.'

Inside, there was already a state of high emotional flux. Barbara, unable to sleep had been watching the quiet countryside of Triopus and had seen the cottage go up in flames. She and Greta had taken lasers from the roof clips and waited for red revolution to break out. Vague distant movement had added to uncertainty. Then the strange car making trips over the blaze brought a climax.

Greta said, 'Did you see that? Against the flame it looked like a body falling in there. What's going on, Barbara?'

'One thing's sure, it isn't Triopus people. They wouldn't use an Earth-type hover car. It must be men from base.'

'That doesn't make sense.'

Barbara Hulse was beginning to have insight where Kirby was concerned. She said slowly, 'Only if somebody arranged an ambush. Commander Kirby has been attacked before. Several times. He's not popular.'

Disaster always seems more likely than success; Greta said, 'This time it's worked out. He and Bob have bought it. Evidence destroyed in the fire.'

'What about us? We're evidence.'

The strange car dropped down beside them to make a period.

'Sure we are. And here come the body snatchers. We're due to be crisped.'

Nothing in the grimed face coming through the hatch offered reassurance and Greta had taken first pressure on the beam release when Barbara recognized Scholes by general shape and size. She was in time to knock up the nozzle and a thin tear whipped along the panel over his head.

He used the time to act for himself and had the laser by its stock before she could re-align.

She was, however, too confused to let go and was drawn

forward, feet together on the ground like a waxwork figure being moved to another part of a tableau.

It was not all that different from moving a cadaver and Scholes, with his hands full, pushed the laser down left so that the body turned and presented him with a head in profile and a refined ear. This he bit delicately in the lobe.

New thinking was prompt and gratifying. Greta stopped bothering about the laser, slipped her arms round his neck and said, 'Bob. You're all right then?'

'I am now.'

Kirby, following up, got a less ecstatic home coming.

'Was it you flying over the fire?'

'Yes.'

'Sending men into it?'

'Dead men.'

'But you are the one with the thing about human rights. What right have you to be an executioner?'

'I ask myself that all the time. You think I ought to settle for being a victim?'

'You could dodge being a victim without turning into a butcher.'

Kirby had a moment of self-analysis which queried why he was never on the receiving end of an uncomplicated welcome. But then, maybe she wasn't the type to deliver that kind of personality flow anyway. Adjustment to living always looked more satisfactory for characters like Bob Scholes and Greta. Perhaps in the long term a depth adjustment was more permanent and satisfying. The question remained whether he would survive into the long term to check out the theory.

As of now, progress in any direction ground to a halt. He said shortly, 'Transfer into the other car,' and set a good example by doing just that.

His going left a social gap. Greta, like an atom with all valences hooked had no time for general exchanges. Scholes with one ear still cocked to the voice of duty got the message and recognized that there was only one way to carry it out. He picked her up and backed through the hatch.

Left alone, Barbara Hulse knew that in her research to get the record straight, she had been less than fair. When you came right down to it, a man had no choice. Stalking the ambush party in the dark had been a military exercise, needing nerve and skill. She ought to have congratulated him instead of sounding off about the morality of it.

She picked up her sling pack and Greta's, looking round the shuttle for anything else they might want and then thought it hardly mattered. A repair team would pull it in. She went slowly out, shutting the door behind her like a prudent house-keeper.

Kirby was already at the console. Much of the floor space was taken up by a machine on its own swivel base. Clearly a directional device with a beam projector. There was no room for doubt about why their own shuttle had come down. As soon as she appeared, the car slammed up in a straight lift and they were off.

Kirby circled once, picked up the course line and accelerated away.

It was a silent ride, with the lights of base camp coming up as a semicircular glow after fifteen minutes. *Cossack* was away on a patrol mission and Kirby had a moment's debate about what to do. He had imagined going straight back to his own ship and talking to Hadden from a position of strength. Still he would not alter a small preliminary which he had thought up.

When they touched down under the canopy of the admin block, they still carried with them an aura of night and distance like late tourists pulling in at a hotel.

The night duty man in reception opened his mouth with a question that was never made flesh. Kirby said, 'Come outside.'

On the way he picked up two riggers passing to join a late shift. Even then it was hard work for five men to manhandle the beam device out of the car and carry it through to Hadden's office.

He left it on the executive desk, flattening a 'pending' tray to a mash, with its snout pointing down to Hadden's chair. A clear illustration of the maxim that whoever invents a weapon must expect to have it used against himself

Back in the hall, he said, 'Wrap it up there, Bob. Take a spell and wait for *Cossack*.'

Greta said, 'Come over to *Europa* and wait in comfort.'

She was including both, but she was looking at Scholes and Kirby had an anti-social fit of pique. He was dog tired and felt bleakly that the present and future both had narrowed down to an empty set. They could have Triopus, fill it with continuous city building, import every feature of Earth economy and rot in a midden of their own creating. They were welcome and if Hadden succeeded in sending him into oblivion it could only be gain.

He said, 'Okay, Lieutenant. You're on pass until *Cossack* comes down. See you.'

Barbara Hulse opened her mouth to speak, but like the desk clerk found frustration; he was gone through the door.

Outside, he skirted the waiting shuttle and went along the main street of Dawson City. Underfoot was trampled remnants of blue grass and bare patches of powdery grey soil. A small dawn wind cooled his damp clothing. Under the street lights, he could only see the sky as a black mask with one white moon in vision.

There was nobody about, but work was going on behind every frontage. He felt better walking in the open and cut through a quarter of dormitory blocks towards the village.

Just before the ground rose to a sloping border of bushes, there was a wide patch without grass, where a digger had cleared the topsoil to get foundations for building. The new level was only half a metre down and hard rock.

Kirby jumped into the excavation and tested it. It was like

a lava flow. Blue glass sheen. Fused under terrific heat and pressure. It reminded him of something and he stood looking at it and at the turned back soil heap.

The soil was crumbly without organic content, a kind of pumice dust. An unlikely medium for any kind of plant growth. More like a mechanical anchorage for roots than a source of nutrients. Could it be that the villagers kept it going by feeding? Soilless culture on a grand scale? But then, they had not seen it in action, and it would surely take regular maintenance to keep it going.

The relays clicked over and he remembered where he had seen a similar rock surface. It was a by-product of nuclear fission. Inner ring. Directly below an exploding bomb where rock melted into this.

So Triopus could have a long history of man-made devastation. If that was so, the elusive Triopusians might be very subtle fish indeed, with more development forgotten than the Earthman had yet dreamed about.

He climbed back to the path and went on, away from the lights. Now he could see the night sky, with darkness thinning out and the glittering blob that was *New World* stationary overhead. A bright speck separated out. *Cossack* was pulling away to continue her tour.

He went on along the canal, past the last of the houses allocated for official use and took the next one in line. The door was wide open and he went inside.

Like all the others, it was quiet and still with a scent of verbena. He lit a resin torch, stripped off and washed in the ewer of warm water. With the door wedged, he stretched out on the bed.

Some kind of optimism was coming back. On the credit side, he was alive. In a universe which was predominantly dead, that had to be a good thing in itself. He saw, as a truth, that the struggle in every man's mind was to fit into the pattern as it appeared to himself. Accept limitations. Know that he could not have all the women, all the food, all the artefacts. Social stability followed when enough people believed, rightly or wrongly, that they had a reasonable share or when some theoretical consideration like religion or duty persuaded them that it didn't matter either way. Seconds later he was asleep.

Farther down the village street, Barbara Hulse, dropped at her home door by taximan Scholes, followed the same behaviour pattern. She spent a few minutes wondering where Kirby had gone and a few more in what she should report to Maynard about the trip.

When finally she went to sleep, however, it was Kirby's restless personality which was on her mind. Some of the questions he kept asking had no simple answers. Although it was uncomfortable, she knew that she did not want him to stop asking them. One thing they should do for sure was check out the moons. And even with misgivings about extra vehicular activity, she wanted to be in the party that went to do it.

Grant Kirby reported direct to Maynard from the video in his own control cabin. He had wakened like a cat at the sound of *Cossack*'s retro bringing her down and was over at the pad before she had stopped flexing on her jacks.

Maynard was not looking pleased. Hadden had already told him that the fact-finding mission was home and dry. Public relations charm was only a thin veneer when he said, 'There you are, Commander. I was expecting you to report in person.'

'I hope you were.'

'What am I to take that to mean?'

'If it means nothing, that's fine. The mission was a failure. Whoever had been in the village had gone. We found nothing. Today I propose to make a search on one of the moons.'

'What do you hope to gain by that? We have reports that *Europa Nine* checked out the moon satellites and found them uninhabited.'

103

'That I know. We did an orbital search and the scanner pictures were negative. No very close investigation was made and I think it is necessary. It is at least possible that something was overlooked. They could be the source of the interference we are getting.'

'That's very unlikely.'

'There are a lot of unlikely things going on.'

'This will have to be approved by the council. *Cossack* can not be put at risk. This could wait until the main force is here.'

'If there is a danger, the main force might never arrive.'

'One of the freight and exploration ships could be used.'

'I will take it.'

'I repeat that is a matter for the council.'

Kirby suddenly lost patience. 'Look, Maynard. In my judgement it is necessary and soon. Get your council to agree it, if you like, but one way or another it will be done today.'

'You realize, Commander, that when the main force is here I shall have to put in an unfavourable report about your interpretation of your role here?'

'If and when. Just now there is no other military force.'

'Controller Hadden will detail a crew if the project is agreed.'

'I'll use the same crew as before. You can send an observer.'

Maynard avoided a direct answer. 'There is a routine conference at eleven hundred. I will let you know what is decided.'

'Do that. I'll be ready to go at 1400.'

Maynard saved face by switching out first as though turning off a hireling shepherd. But the expression he allowed himself, out of range of the viewing eye, was one that no man with a shaven head and a care for his public image would want on an election bill.

Hadden, on the close-range, receiving end of it, took it as a useful indicator of one side of Maynard which he had not reckoned enough. The sex angle was not a sure-fire winner with this one. Power was the thriving motive behind the governor. Threaten him there, and you had him on a raw spot. So far, he had seen Kirby as a temporary nuisance who could be managed. Now he knew it was a direct confrontation.

Never slow to exploit a useful lead, Hadden said, 'You see, Governor, Kirby is a dangerous man. No enterprise can have two directors. He's been lucky so far. But he can't go on being lucky. Not for ever. As a matter of fact, he's gone right outside the law now. You could arrest him under the civil code. Only one penalty too, at this stage of a new colony.'

'He has some supporters. I don't want to have him in court sounding off like an ombudsman. Your way is better. If you can make it stick. Use any method you like. Get him off my back.'

'I'll make it stick. Let him go on this moon trip. Gives me time to get something set up. When he's due back, I'll see that *Cossack* is out on a mission. That way he'll have to come into town to wait for his ship. This time there won't be any mistake.'

Maynard had used the time to reset his face in its bland, executive look. He said, 'Very well, Controller. I'll leave it with you. Take any men you like.'

At the conference, Maynard looked hard at Barbara Hulse when she claimed a place in the moon shot. If Kirby was interested there then it was another good reason to see him off. In the interim, it would keep him under observation if she did go. On a professional level, she was a good witness. Make him feel that the administration had accepted his ultimatum with as good a grace as might be.

He said, 'That would be a good idea. I'm sure the committee are glad of your interest in this, Dr Hulse. Are there any objections to that?'

An hour before his deadline, Kirby had his crew and was checking out *Europa* for a direct run to the moon currently crossing the horizon line. He was, for his part, glad of another mathematician to stand in for the unreliable course data computers and put her in with an official placing at Communications Three with Greta in at two and Pearce, *Europa*'s exec, leading the section.

When he joined the ship with Scholes and Railton half an hour before blast-off, Renshaw had it all buttoned up, with personnel waiting in their couches and preliminary checks made. There was nothing to keep them. Kirby said, 'Let's go then,' and shoved down the red lever to bring in final phase count down. Urgent bleeps began to sound through the freighter as she balanced herself on a thrusting arrow of fire.

Barbara Hulse had not spoken directly to him, but he was aware of her voice on the general net, pushing corrections to Greta and Pearce. Very level tones, seemingly unmoved. Remembering her attitude to weightless travel, he wondered how she really felt. On the whole, it was impossible to know what another person felt about anything. You could only project your own experience. Pain is true if you feel it. The same could be said of pleasure. Communication had an uneasy basis. Perhaps it was never really possible?

Europa was coasting now and navigational problems crowded in. He dropped into the routine of question, answer, correction, bringing them round in a long dropping curve for their objective. There was no room for anything else in his mind.

Sited rear and left of the command console, Barbara Hulse took a half minute, when pressure was off, to watch him at work. Sure and positive in his movements, like an extension of the machine. Spiky and difficult to know; but an individual. One who was not going to be swamped by the system. She was a split second late answering Greta and he was on to it like a hound dog. 'Wake up *Communications Three.*'

Caught in the act, she felt herself blushing inside her silver carapace, something she had not done for some years past. Guilt made her severe. 'The swine,' she thought, emotionally, for a mathematician. 'The *murderer*. I'll get even with him for that.'

Statistical likelihood of any opportunity to do it in the flesh took a knock when *Europa* began to home on its target moon.

Lunar landscape filled the scanner. Bleak, silver-grey, pock-marked with meteoric crater forms. Kirby, working like a robot caller, was taking the ship entirely on manual, asking for distance calculations only from the sonar probes. Pearce broke in urgently, 'Hold that, Commander. Readings all to hell.'

It was like taking a full-rigger on a lee shore and finding that the man shouting 'Mark Twain' had caught a shark on his lead.

Every navigational aid went into a spasm with dials taking a roulette spin. *Europa* was running wild, in a dive that would take her in a tunnelling bid for the moon's core. Even internal communication was blanking out.

Kirby had a split second to think that they had scored a bull's eye on the seat of the jamming interference. Whether the other moons were involved or not there was no longer any doubt about this one.

He used the last failing decibel of sound to get through to Rogers, his Power Exec, and called for full retro. There were two seconds, with the moon surface granulating on the scanner and G building to an intolerable, crushing burden in every acceleration couch, before the ship came round and began to check. Then they were falling again into a dense cloud of metallic ash as the thrust churned out its own, private crater.

He could only leave it to the automatic compensating gear in the tail to sort out an approach speed.

Direct vision ports told them nothing, the scanner was a silver blank. Barbara Hulse had a vision that the moon itself was a mirage, a ball of gas. They would go through it and be out again into clear space.

Then *Europa* found solid rock with a definitive jar that brought every crewman straining against his straps.

Kirby said, 'Report.' But it got no farther than the inside of his own visor. Communication was a dead duck.

Europa struggled back to her full height on two jacks. A tell-tale working on stone-age mechanics showed that she was thirteen degrees out of true. An invisible leaning tower.

Kirby was first out of his clips and orientated at a deeper level than service logic made a first call to see how Barbara Hulse had made out.

She was still lying there, waiting like a good subordinate to be told the next thing. When he looked directly into her visor as one fish to another in neighbouring aquaria, she looked pale and composed like a figure on a catafalque. Her hair had been taken back into the dark cowl of her suit and her face, without make-up, was working for itself as a statement of form. Mathematically precise and satisfying.

It was like diving into confused water and coming up with a head of Aphrodite.

He selected a one-to-one cord from the ravel on her chest and plugged himself in. 'It's okay. Some damage to the ship; but we're down. Are you all right?'

'Yes. What do we do now?'

'Give it time to settle, then we'll have a look round. There's something here, not a doubt.'

'Can we tell them at base?'

'No dice. Complete blanket. Unhook yourself.'

He missed out Greta, next in line, who was sitting up and waiting with her extension line held delicately between finger and thumb for anybody who wanted to know. To Renshaw he said, 'It looks like tripod-two gone. Can you fix it?'

'It depends what we're standing on.'

'Okay. Get your people busy on the repair. I'll take Scholes, Railton and Dr Hulse and have a look at the countryside. Lift-off's no problem if you can get her up another five degrees. We can pull in to *New World* and get it straightened up there.'

'Will do. Take Greta along and do me a favour.'

Twenty minutes later, they were leaving the main lock with Renshaw and his Power section working fifty metres below on the bed of a saucer-shaped pit. Stark and clear now, *Europa* was a fantastic addition to the arid lunar view. Leaning crazily from her hollow nest she looked like a space-age folly.

Linked on a continuous line and using propulsion packs, Kirby's party jetted to a cushioned landfall a hundred metres outside the ring on a surface of pumice dust.

Walking slowly, with controlled steps, he set a pace to keep them moonbound. Wreaths and spirals of fine powder rose to waist height.

From the direct vision port on *Europa* they looked like wraiths in a dream sequence.

Last in line, Greta turned too suddenly to wave to the gallery and corkscrewed into full view at the end of her tether. They were dwindling in middle distance before she was stabilized and back in station.

Only able to speak to her neighbour in line, she said to Barbara, 'What are we doing here? We must be crazy.'

No immediate answer was possible because the one-to-one link was in urgent use by the man in front. He was hauling himself back from a ten metre wide crevasse and wanted everybody to know.

Chapter Seven

From the long elliptical observation deck of *New World 2*
Dr Martinez had a panoramic view of his hurrying empire.
Total satisfaction was, however, denied. There was a bug in
his galactic ointment.

Aesthetics was only a minor part of it; though he had to
concede that the functional transports made no kind of showing against the silver freighters and corvettes spaced out among
the convoy.

After the technical miracle of moving ninety tanks to RV
on the same course, he had falsely supposed that it was all over
except for counting off the days. Even space ought to call him
uncle. But any music in the spheres was taking a long bar rest.

Silence, claimed to be golden, was mere dross. They were
two days within the zone where messages from the advance
party could be expected and nothing yet had come up. It was
as though Maynard's party had set up an Indian rope trick.

A measure of his preoccupation could be taken by any
psychological observer, when a trim red-head came up the
broad stairway from the operations well, moving lithely and
carrying a handset video. In a bronze leotard, with a narrow
silver filigree belt, she was Everyman's space mate and knew it
well. All she got from the leading citizen was a snappish query,
'What is it?'

No life is free from care, she tossed her head in a move that
sent shock waves through the elastic bell of hair and delivered
a plain tale bluntly, 'Squadron Controller Powers for you,
Governor.'

She put it on the arm of his chair and undulated off to
where she was appreciated and Martinez had another cross.

He had been glad enough when pressure from the Lasmec organization, through Wilkes, had kept Halsall from bringing out his squadron. Powers was a safe man. No likelihood there of opposition to colonization plans. But safe subordinates are bought at a price. This one covered himself at every turn by bringing too many details to the top for decision.

The face in the palm-size video was long and fixed in a permanent grimace of big yellow teeth. Known as Horsey Powers in the lower echelons of his command, he had a nervous tick which caused him to click his massive choppers in a double beat as a striking-up to any sentence.

He said, 'Tk. Tk. There you are Governor. Tk. Tk. I've been thinking. Tk. Tk. This radio silence should be investigated. Tk. Tk. I have it in mind to detach a corvette to go forward and investigate.'

Martinez, stroking his forehead, thought, 'Why doesn't the man use longer sentences. Once he's off he ought to keep going. Save time all round.' Aloud he said, 'I'll leave that to you, Commander. It is worrying, of course, not to hear from the advance party; but I have every faith in Dr Maynard. However, nothing would be lost by an investigation. How long would it take a fast ship to go ahead and make the return trip?'

Powers, translating officialese into service terms, recognized that the man meant to say 'Check'. But he went along with the word play. 'Tk. Tk. I have a very special unit, only recently in service. Tk. Tk. She can double the speed of the convoy. Tk. Tk. With a day stop on Triopus, she could still give a useful margin.'

'Very well. Set it up.'

'Tk. Tk. Check.'

Martinez was still watching, fifteen minutes later when the corvette *Gurkha* accelerated away. It was a sight that brought every free man and woman to the observation decks on the transports. Arrow slim, moving out like a comet with an iridescent tail. He listened on a monitor to a beam tap dropped at random in a workshop in *New World 17*. Sampling for indicators of morale.

'Where's she off then?'

'Recce most like. See that the flamin' place's still there.'

'It better had be.'

'What's the use? We can't turn back.'

'Who wants to turn back? This lot could manage, if it never made a landfall. There's the convertors. Protein banks. I reckon we could go on for a thousand years.'

'You could, mate. Not me. I want to get my feet on a drop of hard ground.'

'What for now? What could you do on the ground that you can't do here? What does it matter where you are? You've got enough to eat, haven't you? A bed? There'll only be the same women when we get there. I reckon if you can settle there, you could settle here.'

'Come off it. It's not the same.'

'It's the same anywhere, mate.'

'God, if you can't see that, it's no good talkin' to you. There's one thing that's for sure.'

'What's that?'

'There'll be a credit stoppage on you and me both if we don't get back to the section. There's a whole flamin' bay to bolt up on this shift.'

Martinez switched out. Average stuff. Neither good nor bad. Nothing to pass on to security, though one had seemed dangerously near deviant opinion. On the whole his township of a hundred thousand was in good heart. Actualizers, with hundreds of first-class shows to put on, took care of most of the free time. Work was the great therapy. It had been a good piece of forward thinking to leave most of the construction work for the first satellite to be done on the journey. Everybody had a job. Disaffection could only grow in idleness.

He was feeling more satisfied and turned away from the direct vision shield. Time for a meal. That was a considerable pleasure in itself. He collected Sally Maloon and Glen Watkins from a deep, private conversation on a neighbouring bench seat and moved on with urbanity restored.

Come to think there was something in what that prole had said. They could very well carry on indefinitely. Making and remaking the inside of the transports, joining them together in an infinity of patterns. Generations could succeed one another, the purpose of the mission could be lost, but life would be there, like a self-multiplying cell waiting for something to turn up.

It was a thought to share with his companions; but they were off again in one of their shorthand conversations. Not such a good choice of personal assistants. He sat stroking his forehead and working out a combination which had just occurred to him to bring something novel out of the meal dispenser in the top people's dining suite.

Simultaneously, on Triopus, Defence Minister Hadden was dialling a frugal meal from a temporary dispenser in the committee dining bar at the admin office block. Frontiersmen live rough and the restricted table of twelve variables was beginning to underline the nobility and self sacrificing nature of his great contribution to colonization. Lasmec owed him a lot. When it was all settled up, he was set to take the first freighter back with a claim for compensation of loss of living time.

Since the arrival of the cannon on his jotter, he had recognized that his own survival to make that trip was contingent upon getting Kirby out of the way. He had just spent one hour fixing it good and he felt that he deserved more than a nut cutlet.

Maynard came in, stopped once or twice with other committee members for routine image building and came to anchor at the same alcove table. He dialled at once, with decision, as though fuel was fuel and what the hell. When it was delivered, a steaming mound of anonymous nutrient with banana flavour, he began to load it in with a fork.

Fifty grammes on, he said, 'What arrangements have you made?'

An unseen guest at the table might have asked for more detail, but Hadden had no doubts. 'Enough to settle Kirby for good. *Cossack* is being held from routine patrol until we see *Europa* coming in. Then she'll go. There's a guard detail at the pad. As soon as she's down they'll go aboard to check fuel and stores and keep the ports open. Kirby'll be invited to come in and report to your office. If he does, there's a party of six security men to pick him up. If he doesn't, the guard at the pad will take him.'

'If he leaves the ship and does not report to my office?'

Trust Maynard, thought Hadden to try to pick a hole in anybody else's dispositions. 'That's all right, too. There will be two parties of six in the streets ready to hunt him down. It's a long time since that was a regular feature of Earth justice. The proscribed man—killed in the open. It'll give the workers a break. Morale's good; but no harm comes from an occasional circus and a good example of the wisdom of conformity for all to see. You will have to sign the proscription writ.'

Maynard looked doubtful. It was the only element of the report that struck the wrong chord. 'That is why the practice is in disuse.'

'Why?'

'Signing such a writ puts the finger on the magistrate who does it. In common law, he can be prosecuted by the victim's heirs and made to justify the grounds. Very few magistrates could afford to lose such an action.'

'It's not likely to come to it. That's the third line of defence. But you'd never get anybody taking that up out here. Not that Kirby has any family that I ever heard of.'

'When the main party arrive, we come under full legal

114

constitution. There'll be an enquiry and there'll have to be a report.'

'He's put himself in the wrong all along the line. You don't have to worry.'

It was the wrong words to use to Maynard, 'I don't *worry*, Controller. I don't have to *worry* about anything. You have to worry though. Remember I've seen the Lasmec file, you've bungled the job twice. A third time would make the organization revise its opinion on your value.'

Hadden thought that it was just as well that everything did not get to the personal files and wondered briefly if there was anything about Maynard which might be filtered back by other channels. 'I see the importance of this, Governor. You can rely on me.'

He pushed aside the remnants of his nut delight and left Maynard methodically clearing another swathe with his busy fork.

In his office there was a memo that Mowat was asking when it would be clear to take *Cossack* on patrol. That could wait for a second enquiry. Kirby had been gone six hours. Give him another six, then things should begin to move. He left orders to be called every half hour with a sit. rep. and went along to his own suite in the A living block.

One of the nurses from the medical unit was due to meet him there when she came off duty at seventeen-thirty. Even with the scarcity value to foster dreams of grandeur, she had been flattered by his interest. It was well seen that he was second man in the hierarchy and would be a big power in the colony. Status-wise it would be a fair jump. From level C, upper-technician grade to level A executive. Competition would increase when the main party got in, so she was trying to make herself indispensable.

When he arrived, she was already prudently in bed resting her feet after a busy day in the hospital. Dark hair spread in a symmetrical fan on the pillow, khol-rimmed eyes wide and round, she said with a lisp that grated on his ear, 'I got away early. There wath only one cathualty today. A poor thteel erector got himthelf thquothen between two girderth. He wath tho thwuathy that Doctor Thpenther thaid "Write him off. You'd need a crystal ball to thort that lot out." Tho it thaved uth a lot of time.'

'Well it's an ill-wind that blows nobody any good.'

'What doth that mean?'

Hadden, with a certain self-pity, recognized that Sylvia had been a doubtful choice. She was one of that unimaginative band who had to tell a tale right through without missing out a single detail. Nothing he touched was turning to gold these days. With a busy night ahead, he felt that he could not afford to be distracted. He said, 'Look. I've got work to do. Something unexpected has turned up. When's your next free evening?'

'Not till Thaturday.'

'Well run along, and I'll see you then. Business before pleasure, you know.'

Ambition makes for flexible attitudes. She switched off a sulky pout and swung long legs lithely out of the nest, standing revealed in a short pink slip and minimal triangular pants. He watched gloomily as she wriggled into medical corps coveralls, breasts moving sympathetically like round-backed fish in a silk net.

But Defence Ministers are men of steel at the call of duty. It was just another score to settle with Kirby and that would not be long delayed. When she had gone, he called round the complex to check that his forces were no station. Then he poured himself a long whisky simulate, and settled down to wait.

The object of the exercise would have been pleased to know that he was keeping Hadden waiting. But it would have been the only pleasure to be gained from a negative situation.

After an hour's outward stint, using rocket packs to cover

116

more ground, Kirby passed back the signal for return. Except that electrical and magnetic flux was uniform and intense, there seemed to be no evidence to be won from the moon's sterile crust.

There was no sign of any installation having been ever present. Craters were naturally made. No man-formed artifact was lying about to stumble on.

At the crevasse, with *Europa* in clear view ahead, he stopped again. It was the only uncommon feature on the landscape.

Kirby spoke to Scholes, 'What line have you?'

'Two hundred metres.'

'Give me the shackle. I'll go down.'

Four grotesque heads over the sill watched him float slowly into the gap.

Twenty metres down, the ten metre width had funnelled to a bare three with the facing wall showing strata like an archaeologist's borehole. Changes in rock formation followed a colour code to which he had no key; but now there was a clear difference from the fused volcanic layers of the surface.

He fended off from the sloping wall and used a hand vibrator from the tool kit in his belt to score the stone. It was blue-grey and had a texture like granite.

Scholes was steadily running out line and he dropped another twenty metres in a chimney of uniform width. From above, the bottom had been lost in darkness and had appeared to lie at the foot of this narrow stretch, but when he reached it there was a further drop, with the canyon widening all the way, hourglass in section, and no positive floor to identify.

Beyond the narrow neck, the overhang threw shadow and the far walls were in darkness. He drifted down into the underworld for another fifty metres and then signalled for a stop.

Although insulated from change by his corrugated suit, Kirby had a sense that there was no cold chill in this place. Why he knew it, he could not have said, but it came as no surprise at all when he checked heat gauges and found that had risen two degrees from surface temperature.

There was a vitality which was absent from the moon's surface. As though, here, below the dead crust, the asteroid was still a living thing. It was like being lowered into a dielectric which was under stress of a high potential difference. He could imagine lines of force picking their way through his molecular structure. A penetrated man.

Light from the built-in torch in the crown of his visor sent a white splash roaming along the distant rock face. It appeared to be smooth, faintly rose-pink; uniform as though quarried by hand. Bending his head, he shone straight down and found a solid floor, thirty or forty metres on.

It was littered with debris in a long ridge below the opening. Reckoning that only a few fragments would fall in a decade, the chasm, like the abbess of fiction, must have been yawning for many millenia.

He picked his way down a fantastic slope, with knife-edged fragments lying at gravity-defying angles by Earth standard. In the shifting column of light from his torch, every colour in the spectrum came up in a kaleidoscope spin. An underground mountain of broken glass.

Now he was standing on the side opposite to the anchor man and looking up could see a thin line of bright light at the rim and what could be their heads looking down.

Speech circuits were totally dead. He aimed for the centre blob and used the ancient, emergency light signal system for communication. 'Have reached rock bottom.'

Just discernable against the light, a small yellow dot blinked out, 'Check.'

Then he was looking with unbelief at the wall twenty metres in front of him.

The small circular pool of light from his headset had come to rest on a figure in bas relief which could have been a Triopusian girl lately-gathered, quick-frozen and propped in a niche.

Colour was perfect, as in life. She was wearing a knee length kirtle of fine linen, semi-transparent, so that an opaque triangle of crimson briefs could be seen beneath. A narrow belt of diamond-shaped links in glowing bronze. Over the shoulders, falling away into the stone, a brocade over-mantle. Dark hair brought forward in one lustrous ringlet to vie with Rapunzel's.

She was exactly like many of the women he had seen on the first expedition. He moved the light on and found that it was a long tableau. Men and women. As if on a pilgrimage. A continuous mural, depicting all the activities they had seen on Triopus, and also with a sense of a great procession moving towards some longed-for goal.

He began to signal again. Slowly with pauses for Scholes to acknowledge. 'Found something. Anchor line. Come down one at a time.'

He felt the line respond to a moving weight and he pulled it taut, so that the traveller could come straight in to ground level and miss the coloured glass barrow. It was Railton and the extra light he brought now showed the frieze at two points like roving spots on a crowded dance floor.

When they were all down, there was enough light to see that the panel was five metres high. The figures were exactly life-size and moved on a road beside a canal. In the background was the countryside of Triopus with every colour exactly represented by an inlay of matching stone.

What they could see, must have taken many years to execute and it was only part of a vast spread.

Greta Scott plugged in to Barbara and said, 'It's as though they wanted to represent every man and woman who ever lived on Triopus.'

'Perhaps they did.'

'How do you mean?'

'A way of making each one immortal. Fixed for all time in stone just as they were.'

'I'll tell Bob that.'

She went off on her educating mission and Kirby replaced her on the link.

'What do you think of it?'

'Is this what they were like?'

'Yes.'

'It's no surprise you were to protect their interests.'

'Not that alone. Just look at their faces. It's very likely that we are going to be the ones in need of protection. Even this display makes a point. It's a technical marvel quite apart from any art value. Think of the number of workers involved and the equipment. It must have been done without natural atmosphere, this asteroid's been dead for a long time. Always was I should say.'

The logistics angle made its impact on the expert. 'That means regular supply craft from the planet. But there's no evidence there of space technology. Where are they going?'

It was a question that had to be answered. The artists who had planned the work had built in a sense of urgent and happy excitement. The great crowd was pressing forward to some cosmic hand-out that fed back delight. A queue to end all queues. Whatever it was, an eternity of waiting would not be too long.

Kirby unlocked the shackle and hitched the guide-rope to a glittering viridian spar. In a box canyon with only right and left it couldn't be hard to find it again. He said, 'We'll go along with them and see where they're off.'

He slipped the speech link and mimed for the rest to follow up.

Returned to isolation in her own shell, Barbara Hulse thought that he spoke about them as though they were real people and it was a feeling that was difficult to miss. No representational art she had ever seen had come anywhere near the accuracy and impact of this. It was as though a stroboscope had halted a moving column for a viewing eye, holding a still in counterpoint to real movement which was going on below its surface.

With a kilometre notched up on his trip distance gauge, Kirby stopped again. Although the picture was subtly different and the people were not the same, they might have been anywhere along its length.

On the right, the eternal mural, on the left, the long hill of multicoloured rock. Dim cleft going on beyond the range of torch beams.

The column telescoped to a halt behind him. Four pairs of eyes glittering behind visors in the light of his beam made their own dumbly eloquent point. Nobody wanted to leave it without finding what it was all about.

Privately he set a limit. Give it another kilometre, then back to ground level. Check with Renshaw on the operational possibilities of *Europa* and then go along the surface of the rift valley on the loading trolley. Test drops every five kilometres to see what was going on below.

The others saw him stop as though he had walked into a wall and recoil as the energy absorbed in deforming his suit was given out again in reverse motion.

It was a neat, set piece of ergonomics and Barbara Hulse, following up, walking blind with her eyes on the tableau, got his broad back squarely on her chest.

Greta, trailing last in line, saw the developing comedy sequence and sidestepped Scholes as he took the last of the shock-wave. She was able to kneel down beside him and peer into his visor with her light boring down like a surgeon's spot lamp.

She mimed unmistakeably, 'What are you doing on your back?'

Scholes mimed, 'What are you doing up there? 'and saw the puzzled look as she wondered whether or not she had got it right. While her attention was rivetted by this Semantic ploy, he uncoupled her from the chain gang, took one end of her

121

spring-loaded safety tether, planted both feet on her abdomen and launched her into individual flight.

Greta took off to the end of the line like a weather balloon, the light from her visor falling as a narrow yellow pole.

Transparency was total. Except by touch the barrier could not be discerned. Torch light went through without reflecting. The marching column went on unchecked.

Spreading out, they checked from the wall, where the screen dovetailed into the procession without making any gap, to the foot of the splintery scree. There, the change was dramatic. The invisible shield cut off the long hill like a falling shear. From that point on there was a stretch of empty floor, clear and polished with its surface engraved in an endless tesselation of hexominoes.

Greta, who had been content to drift overhead, found that she had gone ahead of the party. She pulled on the rope to alert Scholes and he in turn knocked on Kirby's visor.

The anchoring line went up straight for seven or eight metres to an invisible corner and made an angle. Greta was over the top of the cleared area.

She made the same assessment and began to haul back on the line until she could stand on the roof. To make the point, she did a small shuffling dance in the circle of light from the turned up headlamps.

Kirby thought, 'There is something in some human beings that deserves better than it gets. Here she is, as bizarre a setup as you could get, isolated, at the end of a cord like a puppet, as far from her natural habitat as a biological specimen could well get; but she's still an individual person with a sense of occasion.'

He plugged in on the one-to-one link with Scholes and said, 'Bring your friend down, Bob. Search every centimetre of this wall.'

'What are we looking for?'

'A lock, what else? There has to be a way of getting inside or it doesn't make any sense.'

'That's the understatement of the century.'

Barbara Hulse found it, when he had already looked twice at his time disk and reckoned that they could not allow more than five more minutes. If *Europa* did not blast off before the satellite spun away from facing *Triopus*, they were stuck with it for another eleven hours for the night to pass. Navigational problems in the current stone-age, dead-reckoning phase would be too great for a lift off from the dark side.

She had been waving for some time before she attracted his attention, unwilling to leave her find in case she could not locate it again. When Kirby broke her isolation by the direct speech channel, he could hear the excitement crackling in her voice. 'It's a recess. A hand grip, I think. But what it does, I don't know.'

'Let me try it.'

Kirby hooked his fingers into a niche ten centimetres long by four or five wide. Undercut to make a grip. Barbara had been trying to slide a panel left or right, but it occurred to him that for an action of that kind, there would be no need to have the socket cut back. Why was it designed in that particular way? There would be a good reason.

He stood back and pulled gently towards himself and the answer was plain. Moving effortlessly, as though a technician had only just completed the installation, a large panel came away and began to lift. Up and over like a hangar door on Earth planet.

They went through into a ten metre square room. As they checked out the walls and found it to be so, Barbara working back along the wall where the entrance was, found a continuous surface again. She covered it twice, running a gauntlet along the smooth glass panelling. Talking to herself aloud inside her suit she said, 'But it was just here. I *know* it was just here.'

An etiolated whisper from her outside speaker penetrated to her nearest neighbour like a ghost voice. Kirby spoke for himself. Strangeness was a catalyst for a sudden intimacy between them as though they were long-established friends. 'I heard that. What is it, Barbara?'

'Grant. I can't find the doorway.'

He was checking pressure gauges. For speech to carry, there would have to be an atmosphere. It was there too, coming up all the time. When he spoke again she got it loud and clear.

'It's an atmosphere lock. There's enough pressure now for normal breathing.' He filtered a sample through a metering slot on his chest console and read off percentages. 'It's Triopus atmosphere.'

'I'll be glad to get this off,' she was already tugging at the seals below her visor.

'Hold that,' his voice fairly cracked out in the enclosed space and the other seekers stopped their research and turned his way.

Kirby went on, 'This lock filled in minutes and could empty in minutes. Stay sealed up for the time being. It must take us on to a controlled atmosphere complex or what's the point of it? Look around for the exit.'

After being incommunicado, Greta was a random talker. Arms outstretched in a 'let me out, let me out' mime, her plummy drawl was as bizarre, in the circumstances, as any other single element on the set.

'Looking at those people I'd say there would be more than one way out.'

Scholes humoured her, 'Tell me why, Mr Bones.'

'Too many Basques for one exit.'

Backing her firmly against the invisible wall, he unscrewed her speaker outlet and waved the capsule in front of her visor. Now she was reduced to a listening brief. She said, 'You sneaky, treacherous *rat*, Scholes.'

He got the gist of it; but shook his head like one having reluctant traffic with a nut and she turned away with a slow burn that was effective through two filtering visors. Forgetting the barrier, she walked away from him and was the first to go through into the next apartment.

She even managed to make it look as though she had known all the time the opening was there and Scholes followed through with the speaker component held out as a good-will offering.

Along the whole rear wall, two-metre sections had pivoted on their centres and gave free access to the inside. Sensitive now to sound, they all heard the faint swish of moving air as the louvres closed behind them.

Railton said, 'Two barriers. How do we get out?'

It was left hanging in the air as pure rhetoric. Certainly there was no obvious answer. Now they had the whole floor of the canyon clear and free and swept empty. There was nothing at all which suggested a control panel. The mechanism was working to please itself.

In all the silence and emptiness there was one dynamic. Full of colour and energy the figures on the frieze pressed on to their destination. Nobody looking at it could avoid a wish to join in. Humanity, comfortable in the mass, promising the individual an end to introspective fears.

They crossed the smooth tessellated floor and stood beside the procession. There was such a sense of trust and social solidarity that Kirby broke out the seals of his visor and tipped it back.

After a few long steady breaths, he said, 'It's okay. I reckon in an area this size, it couldn't all disappear fast enough to catch us out.'

Using hand torches, they followed the lines of the frieze, walking beside the people. Except for a whiteness of skin, Greta Scott could have moved over and joined the party with no questions asked. Barbara Hulse, walking companionably with Kirby, made a complete contrast.

There was no question of going back to conform to any time schedule. Whatever happened, they had to know what was at the end of the line; to what green altar they were bound.

The end came unexpectedly, after a good two hundred metres of progress with no material change.

Light, without localized source, flooded the perspex box. It grew until the great bas relief was brilliant with colour; texture of sharp shadow and highlight. Dead ahead, the figures appeared to be walking out of the rock and stood in the round. Free-standing statuary.

It was the head of the column: they had reached the front of the queue.

Kirby was talking to Barbara Hulse as though they were alone.

'I remember once hearing a speech from a visitor to the Initial Training School. High moral stuff. He was on about queues and it stuck in my mind. Pure corn really. Life with a capital L being a queue and you shuffle away with your head down. But gradually it moves on, although you don't notice it and the press up front thins out, so that, eventually, you find you are next in line for whatever it is. It's *your* turn and it comes on a number of issues. Can't be avoided. However you've used your time when you were hidden in the ruck you're on your own now with your problem.'

'Designed to foster dedication. Fill every minute with sixty seconds and all that.'

'Correct. But the old man was right in one respect. It does happen. You do get out in front and you're the only one there and you know that there's only you to do whatever it is.'

They had reached the front of the procession and its leaders were a man and woman. Symbolic Triopusians. There was no doubt that they had been modelled on two people who had been alive. In all, but movement, they were so still.

At the head of the myriad throng in the valley of bones, the two stood hand-in-hand before a column of blue-green glass which ran from floor to ceiling like a squat supporting pillar.

The girl had thrown down her clothes in a heap on the left

and the man had done the same on the right. There was a white kilt and a tunic with interlocking patterns of triangles.

Whatever they were going to face they had to do it without possessions of any kind. But the taut eager lines of their bodies showed there was no hanging back. It was a consummation of free will and spontaneous desire.

Barbara without conscious intention had taken Kirby's gauntletted hand. She said slowly, 'There's only one thing that could make them look like that. They were going to die. That was what they found at the head of the queue. A perfect and satisfactory personal end if that can be. Why should anyone so beautiful find it an acceptable thing?'

Kirby said, 'She *is* beautiful, but no more beautiful than you are. Less, because you are alive and she is dead. We have reached the head of the column now. We have to find out where she went.'

It was not as easy at all that. In the brilliant light the column stopped enraptured at the blue glass shaft. There was nothing else.

They stood round the cylinder like clumsy dancers setting up a maypole. Foreheads against the glass they looked down into its translucent depths. Far below there was a glow of light which began to strengthen.

Greta said, 'It's going brighter.'

'No it isn't. It's coming nearer'—Scholes grabbed for her to pull her away as the growing light reached a crescendo of blue white brilliance like a thousand unscreened welding arcs.

They were on the floor with their faces down. Kirby had his arm over Barbara Hulse and saw that her hair gathered the light itself—molten electrum running in bright liquid into her suit. Then the brilliance dimmed and he was able to look up.

The whole of the inside of the cylinder was taken up by an equilateral pyramid which could be understood as a form although the detail of its structure was beyond all definition. From the apex to the centre of the base was an arabesque of white luminence, source of the light that had blinded them. Still and yet moving. Changing and yet the same. The paradox at the heart of mysticism made flesh.

Barbara Hulse said, 'It *knows*. It's *alive*,' and felt Kirby's arm tighten clumsily over her turtle back.

Chapter Eight

They were standing now. Unbidden, but moved by a common urge to show themselves at their best, they had peeled off the clumsy space gear. There was no imaginable threat in the glowing form behind the glass. If anything, they were fighting an atavistic desire to kneel down in simple humility and wait for instruction.

Kirby said slowly, knowing that speech was unnecessary and that it was only giving belated form to direct thought transfer, 'We are from the far-distant planet Earth. We do not understand what has happened here.'

There was no sound or change in the subtle curving line of the arabesque in the heart of the pyramid, but communication flowed towards them and they could not doubt that an answer had been made.

'Confession of ignorance is the beginning of wisdom. Why should you understand something which was ancient before consciousness began in your world? Even now you are only at the beginning of your psychozoic age. What you see is the end-product of aeons of development. The final move in integration of social structures. The people of Triopus achieved immortality in this form. A concentration of spirit into stability and beauty. The flesh made word.'

Barbara Hulse said, 'Who are the people on Triopus? Where have they gone?'

'They were shadows. Projections of the minds concentrated here. In our eternal life, we people the stage below with actors to live out the life we knew. It is our pleasure to experience life through them. But we have withdrawn them to consider what to do about your arrival.'

'But the houses and the plants and the food.'—Greta had almost lost her drawl.

'They are maintained stereoscopically by continuous energy flow from two of the satellite moons. While it exists it is real in your sense. It was so even before we withdrew to this place. Triopus is very old. The equipment set up there is self-energizing with indefinite life.'

'But if it stops, the planet will be uninhabitable.' Scholes made it a statement; but an answer came back.

'It will not stop. But why should you be concerned? Nothing is permanent in the human situation. Life is lived on a knife-edge between being and non-being.'

It was Berkeley's tree—an idea in the mind of God—and the thought had presented itself to Kirby in a barely coherent flash of insight when it was taken up as though he had put it into overt speech.

'You are right in that. Matter is only energy in a particular form, it is easily organized, though the knowledge to do it is long to achieve.'

Kirby said, 'Why did you send the ships to attack our convoy?'

For the first time there was hesitation in the reply. As though a perfect being found it hard to come to grips with a dissonant imperfection. The glowing pyramid appeared to dematerialize by going in a free fall down its elevator shaft, and they were alone on an empty set.

It left a gap which they felt as the quintessence of human loneliness; as though all the lights in their world had gone out. Barbara Hulse instinctively went close to Kirby and took his arm. She was very near to tears, 'Why didn't they answer?'

She was asking for comfort and he put his arms round her, holding her as one would reassure a child. But the question troubled him and he had no reply.

It came unexpectedly from behind them in their own language, in a voice that was an amalgam of Barbara's and

Greta's accents. 'You will find it more comfortable to talk to us.'

The leading pair in the procession might well have stepped back into life. Two Triopusians were walking towards them and the girl, who had spoken was holding out her hands in the universal mime of goodwill.

Scholes recovering fast, said, 'Export model phantom, mark 1. There's a fortune in it for the right developer.' He added 'Ouch' as a tailpiece, prompted by a smart kick from his neighbour.

Kirby kept his left arm round Barbara's waist. He could feel an involuntary muscular tremor, making her shiver as though there had been a drop to zero. Speaking as much to her as the newcomers he said, 'These are like the people we talked to on the first expedition. Now I know why they spoke with different opinions. They were reflecting the indecision of this mind about the wisdom of allowing us here at all. But I still do not see why they should oppose the colony now. There has been nothing done so far which could cause distrust.'

'Nothing?'—it was the man who spoke now with a similar intonation to Kirby's. 'Nothing you say? You forget that every action on Triopus has been seen. Every conversation monitored. Every half-felt wish and drive has been analyzed. You Earth men have come a fair way along the path of technical progress, but you have outstripped your own personal psychical growth. You have built a house too big for your spirit. There is immaturity, infantilism, violence and selfishness. It is not pleasant for us to watch.'

If the pyramid had made that communication, they would have accepted it without question. But a brown-skinned man in a white kilt and a mantle of coloured cloth, however Apolloesque, was only a man. His partner, who could have sold refrigerators in any part of the arctic circle to stunned male householders, was still only a woman.

Barbara Hulse received it as an astringent, stopped feeling awed and looked indignantly at Kirby.

131

He said, 'All these things may be true; but in spite of this impressive place you have not outgrown violence. The men killed in the convoy came to a painful and unnecessary death because of your actions. If you had made up your mind earlier on and said clearly that you were against the colonization project it might have been halted.'

'That is naïve, and you know it. The man Martinez was determined to represent Triopus as a suitable place. There have been many attempts to silence you as a critic of their plan. But there is something else which you do not know. This is what we have come to explain to you.'

After the emotional strain, the calm voice was an anticlimax. Suddenly tired, Greta sat on her pile of gear. The girl said sympathetically, 'You have been under a great strain. We are sorry. Sit down and rest. I am Comana. This is Tabal. Shall we bring food for you?'

Railton said, 'Ectoplasmic Beefburger with wraith sauce. Thanks, honey. I'll stick to a ration pack.'

Tabal went on, 'When the people of Triopus made this great final move into a perfect unity of spirit, there were some, a few, who could not, finally, bring themselves to forgo the self. Millions came here in the great procession you see and dissolved into the single, but manifold, will. There are sixteen of the pyramid forms. Eight are predominantly of the female principle and eight of the male, though there is no precise end or beginning in that sense, it is a continuum. It is in the interaction of the thought of the sixteen that an infinite variety of interest can come.'

Greta said, '*We* get along. Interest-wise, that is.'

Tabal looked at her, but did not take it up. 'Those who did not join in, withdrew to a small enclave on the fourth moon. The self is self-destructive. They were violent and insecure. Numbers are small, possibly a thousand or less finally settled to a community life.'

Barbara Hulse said, 'Are they still there?'

132

'That is the point I am coming to. They are very advanced in all technical matters, though they have lost a great deal of the knowledge that Triopus once had. It is they who sent the ships to attack you. Two spacecraft remained on that moon from the ancient times when there was a space age on Triopus and our people explored the galaxy. If they had been able to recreate some of the more advanced craft you could not have escaped.'

Kirby said, 'Do they intend to oppose the colony?'

'We cannot tell. Although they have no power to interfere with us, they have built their city complex under such dense insulation that their thought patterns are screened from us. It is likely.'

Barbara Hulse said bitterly, 'So we can't win. Your opposition—if you come down that way—would be enough. This is something else. An evil principle and a good with the evil definitely against us and the good potentially so. And the colony is divided against itself.'

Comana said, 'What will you do?'

Kirby stood up and leaned both palms on the cool glass of the shaft. When he spoke, he was looking into it like a crystal gazer. 'We shall go back and report what we have seen and heard. If you come with us it would help them to understand. There is only one answer as far as the fourth moon is concerned. If they try to destroy us, we must try to destroy them. Primitive by your ethic; but they would understand it. Will you prevent us from doing that?'

'No. But neither would we applaud you if you succeed. Other considerations will finally determine our attitude.'

Barbara said, 'Always on sufferance then. It will be a poor way to live.'

'You cannot understand the nature of the composite mind. It is not simply additive. After a point, complexity brings a new dimension. When we say you would not understand there is no undervaluing of yourselves. This is a simple truth which was not known even to the Triopusians before the fusion took

133

place. Once the right answer has been found, it will be accepted and will be permanent because it will be right.'

Greta said, 'God in sixteen persons, blessed hexadecahedrality—if that's a word.'

Scholes said, 'How filthy can you get? This is high-level stuff, Scott. Outside the scope of a low-minded woman.'

He should have moved first; she picked her spot with some care and kicked his other shin.

The faint bar of light marking the cleft above was still bright. Kirby came to a decision, 'There may still be time to get back now. Can you stop the electrical interference?'

'No. It is part of the nimbus surrounding the composite minds; but the difficulties you have on Triopus are not of our making. It must come from the fourth moon. They could be building destructive forces against you.'

'Shall we see you again?'

'Perhaps.'

Tabal and Comana walked towards the blue glass and appeared to dissolve against its surface. A faint scent of verbena, reminiscent of the houses on Tropius, remained in the square.

Action was better than speech. Kirby picked up Barbara's suit and held it for her. Two minutes later they were ready to go.

Greta said, 'They might have stayed to operate the lock;' but when they reached the wall, the louvres were wide open and they could walk through into the ante-chamber.

As though it was known that speed was important, the pressure began to sink as soon as they were inside and speech was impossible again. Then they were out through the far door and Kirby was looking up to check that it was still light on top.

Time was running out. He saw them hooked up and pointed to the gap. Leaving the guide rope would cut the journey.

Renshaw, with *Europa* buttoned up and ready for a lift-off, saw the bead chain surface as though programmed for an independent flight and held fast on the last phase.

Kirby brought them round in an arc and homed on the ship.

Light levels were falling on Triopus and Hadden was beginning to regret his steel-willed rejection of the path of pleasure. The target moon was almost level with the horizon when justification set in as a tiny asterisk of orange flame. *Europa* had blasted off.

He reckoned an hour would see them home and dry and called Mowat who had been held back for the second time and was not pleased.

Cossack's scanner had picked up the tell-tale light and Mowat said, 'Commander Kirby will be due back. Communication snags are stacking up. I'd like him to see the score. Can it wait?'

'No, captain, it can't wait. In any case, the Commander has had a long mission, he is due for a rest period.'

Concern from that quarter triggered alarm signals in Mowat's head. Screening his voice he asked Tague frankly, 'What's the smarmy bastard working on now, J.B?'

'You'd need a trepanning tool to dig that out. It can't matter much. We'll be back in a couple of hours. Two patrols missed. We ought to go.'

'Okay. I expect you're right.'

To Hadden he said, 'Very well, Controller. We'll fly the usual mission.'

Hadden watched with a plot-weaver's satisfaction as a fire ball began to build and *Cossack* started to nose out into the darkening sky. He poured himself another drink and reached for the video. Even on the short internal run, picture quality was not good and speech was distorted, but it was enough to work by. They were all in place still. All full of sap and promise. Kirby would need to be a fakir to survive this one. Hadden sipped his drink and tapped a simple tune on the arm of his chair with an ivorine stylus he was fond of. He would go along to the office and take personal charge of that end. It would be a pleasure.

Worsening communication was very evident to Kirby as he brought *Europa* through the last atmosphere layer above Triopus. It was a visual judgement job with only experience and fast reaction times to pit against the vagaries of density and thrust. There was also *Europa*'s jury leg to keep doubt hot to the last second.

When she was down, with a feather-light touch that only sank her a half metre on her hydraulic jacks, Renshaw said, 'That rates the top, Commander. She's never made a better planetfall.'

All is relative. In the scanner, *Europa*'s designated pad with its temporary block house and basic gantry looked busy for the time of day. Kirby had been used to flying patrol missions from an empty site and returning to the same. There was a reception committee of at least half a dozen.

Scholes said, 'They're getting very keen to hear what we have to say. Before you know, you'll have a load of *leis* round your neck and an ear full of pollen.'

Kirby said, 'There's nothing yet to set Maynard jigging round the house. The reverse in fact. I have a feeling the pyramids will decide against a colony. When you think it out, you can't blame them. Sooner or later, man here will be a threat. Some researcher will want the credit for unscrambling a composite or for harnessing its power to a coffee mill. They might think they're secure, but a grade one missile down that cleft would split their fourth moon into pebbles.'

Renshaw had run out a coolant. As it cleared, he gave the stand-down for his own crew and flicked down the studs for 'Main Port Open'.

In the scanner, they saw the improvised gantry run up and overlap the sill. Kirby, taking the detail onto a mental file that held the record of a thousand similar moves, saw the difference at once. No regular spaceport gang would do that. As it was, it would be impossible to close the hatch.

Perhaps it was the damaged leg? Losing height fractionally.

He checked the tell-tale and found it reading a full due.

Renshaw had noticed it. 'Will you look at that? The ham-fisted bastards. If I try to seal up with that in place, there'll be a major repair needed. Couldn't be done out here either. It makes you think. God, we've got a crummy lot on this colony. I shall be glad to get out of it for one. That was set right before we left. They only had to move it up.'

The nudge of a sixth sense told Kirby that there was something in it for him. No untrained man would alter the gantry for no reason. It had been changed for a purpose and that purpose could only be to ensure that *Europa*'s front door remained open.

Six men had moved smartly up the chute and appeared on the apron. Suspicion became certainty. They were all armed. All members of the security service which was the Governor's private police force. One stayed on the sill. The others disappeared inside.

At the same time, Hadden came up on the scanner. Interference sent zig-zag tears across his face so that it formed and reformed, flickered from photogenic official to zany psycho. His voice was clear, though. Asking Commander Kirby to be good enough to meet him at his office straight away to discuss something important that had come up; pointing out that *Cossack* was away on a mission; ending on the courteous note that he was sending an escort with a car to save Kirby any further trouble.

Scanner pictures at ground level were suffering even with the huge power of the reactors to punch up the signal. Greta Scott making a spin round the campus before closing down for the night picked up one clear still of a security guard standing at an intersection. Street lighting was on. There was nobody else in sight and no traffic, but he was waiting for something to turn up.

She said, 'What's going on? They've got the gendarmes out.'

Kirby said bitterly, 'Our Defence Minister has set it all up.

He wants to be sure there's only one way to go. This time I report to him at his office.'

There was a tap on the hatch and when it slid back a guard with section-leader tabs was framed in the oval. 'Urgent request from Controller Hadden, Commander. Report to the admin centre. We have a car.'

'Can't it wait?' Barbara Hulse's voice had the confident timbre of a Lasmec executive, 'Commander Kirby can report to the morning meeting of the Council.'

The section leader looked as though he would have been glad to please the first citizen's lady, but had no room to manoeuvre. 'Not possible, Dr Hulse. It has to be now.'

She was already out of her space gear, ready for the shore in white coveralls and sneakers. She said, 'Well we can't spend time now on this report. It's been a long trip. Does Dr Maynard know of this?'

'I believe he does. But you are not required Doctor. Only the Commander.'

Kirby had shrugged off his outer suit. There was no longer any doubt in his mind that Hadden had sprung a neat trap. Without making it obvious, three guards had edged into the narrow confines of the control cabin. They were sited where they could drop Scholes and Railton. If he pushed it to a showdown, there would be casualties amongst the civilians.

He stripped the equipment belt with its heavy-pattern laser from the space suit and buckled it on as he talked. 'That's all right, section-leader. There's no need for anyone else. I'll see Controller Hadden.'

Confirmation that it was more than routine came in the expression on the man's face. He had expected trouble and it was going to be easy. There was relief and yet a certain insolent triumph, as though he had put one over on the military arm.

Kirby stacked one ace in a corner, 'Lieutenant Scholes, contact Captain Mowat when he comes in. Tell him where I am. If I'm not back on *Cossack* in two hours, he can do a little selective target practice on the admin block.' It was said without threat and the hatchet man was prepared to take it as proof positive that even a military man could crack a joke.

'You'll be well away before then, Commander.'

Scholes however took it at its face value. 'Check. We'll take the place apart.'

It was not popular with the non-military security force; but the section-leader kept his smile with an effort that brought small beads of sweat to his forehead.

Ready to go, Kirby spoke last to Barbara Hulse. She too was standing clear of her chrysalid shell. Trim and tall. Hair tightly back so that the broad oval of her head was a statement of form. Mathematically satisfying in the exact proportions of the Golden Section. Brown eyes serious, steady and considering, waiting for him to give a lead.

He knew that if he told her to come along she would follow him. That in fact she was expecting him to do it. But when you got down to cases there was nothing she could do, about whatever they had set up. He did not want her as a witness to his execution.

He kept his voice matter-of-fact, 'Report what you know to the council tomorrow, Dr Hulse. You may be able to influence them. Unless they mount something bigger, *Cossack* can deal with the fourth moon. Good luck.'

Outside, a low level transporter was waiting on its skids. Hadden saw the party leave *Europa*. Two guards down the ladder then their murdered man, two more guards and the section leader. He had done well. Hadden noted his shoulder flash G.57. A man to use again on a tricky assignment.

It was not lost on Kirby. Seated on a centre stall with security men back and front, left and right, he knew well enough he was under escort.

From the oval ports, as the car went through at ground level, he could see that men had been posted at intersections. Hadden was leaving no stone unturned and every one with a louse under it.

He calculated coldly on probabilities. Inside the car, he had no chance. At the entrance porch there would be general movement, shifting vectors, maybe some cancelling of advantage. Once inside Hadden's office he was a dead duck.

Moving his hands without haste, so that there was no misinterpretation of motive, he hooked his thumbs in his belt and sat back as though completely relaxed.

Keyed up and ready to exploit any opening, he had a sudden insight into what was going on. He knew that Hadden was watching the car in. He knew that there were three others in the office with the Defence Minister and three more in the anteroom. In the foyer, there were six and he could tell the directions from the door where they could lay on a line of fire.

It was so clear that he might have been responsible for the plan himself. He sat very still. The pyramids? Their all-seeing eyes would pick up that data. Were they passing it on to him? He ought to be grateful, but first reactions included resentment that he should be so easy of access to the influence of an outside force. Besides, information was not enough. He needed something working for him on the ground.

The car slid under the canopy of the admin block. Street lighting had been good, but this was intense. Floods, battens, footlights, the lot. An empty set without a shadow.

Two men went out first and stood either side. When Kirby ducked through the hatch, they were giving him a metre clearance to save masking anybody's line of sight.

Kirby's right hand was centimetres above the grip of his laser. He straightened up and walked straight forward towards the open doors of the reception area, aware of six converging aims centred on his chest, expecting any second to feel the hot needle thrust of a laser beam making his quietus.

Knowledge of what was there concealed, had its drawback. By now, he would have made his move. On the other hand, he would also have been dead. He was a pace from the door when he knew what the pyramids were going to do. There was time to close his eyes and drop on all fours as the lights cut.

He heard the transparent doors shatter in crossfire over his head and was out of the porch running lightly along by the wall before torch beams began questing about looking for him.

Hadden had a second of pure unbelief. From a neat, straightforward exercise as discreet as security could wish it was now all over the place with all the publicity Kirby could want. He called the duty engineer squad, as emergency lighting came up to a picturesque glow.

To the waiting security men he snarled, 'Get after him. He can't get far. Give it out he's space sick. Tried to assassinate me. There's five hundred credits for the man who puts him down.'

When the engineer-in-charge came up on video, he was so obviously puzzled that there was no point in making anything of it. 'There was a surge. Something like a fifty per cent gain. Safety factor runs at twenty. There was no time to shed any load and we took a burn-out. Five minutes, Controller, and you'll have all the light you want.'

Street lighting came up as Grant Kirby reached the perimeter and put a twenty metre wide ring round the site. Even though Triopus had no wild life, the engineers had followed the regular plan of setting up a light trap with look-outs on every twenty degrees of arc.

After the first week, they had not been manned, but Hadden would have brought them in for a sure thing. Kirby leaned flat against the wall of a freight shed. After a twisting run with much doubling back to miss guards, he was on the far side from the village with *Philadelphia* looming ahead two-hundred metres off on her sylvan pad.

He recognized that he had been lucky. All the way through to this point, he had known what was round the next corner. Twice he had been able to whip into connecting alleys at the very moment that a guard was turning into the end of a street.

With only a dim glow from emergency power and Hadden's special force too small for full coverage, there had been gaps in the net. But this was his seamark.

Either the pyramids were no longer interested, or they had changed their policy for reasons beyond human wit. He felt that he was alone again. He could not tell where his pursuers were. Any second there could be one coming into this staggered radial from the intersection twenty metres back.

Kirby looked across a brightly lit strip. It was tempting to think that he could cross it at a run and have a chance to dodge any fire. But he suppressed that. Now the lights had gone up, he would have to change his plan. Breaking cover was playing into their hands. Even a ham-fisted civilian marksman could swing a self-aligning, mounted laser on to its target. He would be cut to strips before he had gone fifteen metres.

A slow-rising, cold rage began to grow in him. All right, they had him trapped. It was only a matter of time. Instead of going out, he would go in. Work back to the centre and seek out Hadden.

Making the decision conferred a kind of freedom. Now he no longer cared what happened to himself. He would get as near to the admin block as he could go.

The wall behind him was flexible-alloy cladding and he cut a panel out of it with the vibrator at his belt. Inside, there was one arc lamp slung high in the roof and a small group of riggers putting up storage bays. He walked silently behind a row of crates and came out twenty paces from an open door.

The security guard coming through to ask the honest sons of toil if they had seen a man in white, opened his mouth to yell. That and all questions else clotted among his synapses as he fell forward into the shed. Kirby was out before anybody turned round and the foreman, when he was called, genuinely believed the man had died of a stroke. He rang the medical unit for a tender.

Kirby crossed the narrow connecting lane and went straight

142

for the opposite building. In the warm Triopusian night, its double doors were folded back. On this radial, all the first phase buildings were for storage. This one was criss-crossed with spidery catwalks which would eventually be automated as gravity conveyors.

Now they were static. Two men in a sliding cradle were working down from the top with spray guns putting on an anti-corrosive finish. In such a still place anything moving had to be noticed. Kirby walked down the middle of the floor, saw two faces looking down and gave the brief wave of a man passing through acknowledging property rights.

He was ten metres from the far wall when the tannoy gave a preliminary burp and crackled into urgent life. It was Hadden's voice and Kirby's lips writhed back involuntarily.

'Attention. Attention. Citizen action. Commander Kirby has been outlawed for treachery to your colony. He has already killed one security guard. He is dangerous. There is a reward of five hundred credits to the man who brings him in. Dead or alive. Better dead, it would save everybody's time. Be careful.'

The cradle was coming down with both men leaning out avid for glory. Kirby had ten seconds to run a laser beam across the catwalk midway between two stanchions. He saw a gap open up as the weight of the tray fractured the weakened metal and was outside again before they hit the deck.

Anyone plotting a movement graph by reports could interpolate his next, but Kirby no longer cared. With the whole colony against him it could only end one way.

Like the pyramid said, human life was lived on the knife-edge of being and non-being. For him, it had been more obvious than for most; but once he was committed to action he could forget it.

Fatigue was long gone. He was light weight, as though on a low-gravity planet. He felt his shoulders moving flat and muscular inside his coveralls. He was larger than life, invulnerable. The thought came to him that he should take off his epaulettes which alone picked him out as a military man; but a certain pride came into it. He would not step down in any way.

The next building in line was an embryo records terminal. Storage for profiles of the incoming main party and eventually of all new Triopusians. Girls were methodically coding long lines of racking on the standard reference system.

A plump strawberry-blonde had an electric stylus raised for action and her tongue pushed out as an aid to concentration when she saw him through the lattice. Her first yell was triggered off by having bitten into her own flesh, but the second was clear enough. 'It's him. It's that man.'

Tracked by a dozen pairs of eyes from every side, Kirby reached the far end. Out of the tail of his eye, he saw a foreman gathering four riggers, waving them to follow.

They came on with long strips of slotted angle raised like javelins, willing to wound; but prudently afraid to strike.

The door he was making for slid briefly back and closed again. There was just time to see the flash of security insignia. From behind there was a flurry of movement and he saw that three men had come in at a run and were fanning out for cover. A line of shelving beside him suddenly went into collapse.

Even then he did not believe that it could happen to him. He grabbed for an overhead beam, felt a sudden sting in his left side and then was over the edge on to a rudimentary second floor. He took time off for careful aim and carved up a guard who was standing to fire up at him. Then he was climbing like a machine through a fantastic stairway of girderwork.

Down below a dozen guards had come in. Two were man-handling a riot gun from a patrol car. Once they had it set up, they were on a sure thing. Kirby came up to the roof and began to cut himself a manhole. When the metal sagged away he took the circle and skimmed it down.

Expecting any second to be bisected he heaved himself through on to a dark flat oblong above the level of street lighting. Somewhere overhead *Cossack* was making her tour. He looked at his time disk. Not long before she was back. Too long, but not long in an absolute sense. One more illustration of the introspective value put on time.

He went to the edge and looked over. They were looking up against the light and would not see him, riggers, girl operatives, two or three nurses, a growing crowd to see what the cornered man would do.

It was dark on the roof, but he could make out a litter of light alloy girdering ready for the next stage. Looking at the next building in line, he reckoned that the longest beam would reach it with a metre spare either end if he could sway it across.

Pushing it out was no good. He could not get the purchase to keep the end down. Working from one end he stood it upright like a flagpole and edged it to the parapet. Rebound might shake it loose and away, but there was nothing else. He let it go, threw himself across the end to damp out oscillation. Taking the jar of impact through every nerve and bone.

The crash brought them all round at a run, but he was already walking across, a man on the high wire.

Once over, he shoved the end free and heard the panic scatter as it went down. He was not far now from the centre. In fact, this unit was one of five arms branching out from the admin building itself, which stood like a boss in the wheel's centre.

Hadden, checking off reports, picked up the pattern. There was no doubt about it, Kirby was making for the middle again. He went out into the corridor. Two men were on duty with lasers ready drawn. Back inside, he had two more. There was nothing Kirby could do. He was virtually handing himself over on a plate.

The whole place was enclosed except the window. He moved one man to watch that as a full time chore. Then he went through into the washroom behind his executive desk, a totally sealed unit without even an external wall. He saw the brand new hatch in its roof before he saw Kirby, and was trying to get back into the room when a laser beam took him through his left sideburn in a rising line to the top of his head. Black night filled his eyes. His EEG went forever flat.

Kirby, feeling suddenly tired to the point of death, swung himself out again and back to his rooftop. He lay for half a minute feeling the cold metal against his skin, wondering that he was still an identity; a discrete form with a certain past, a present and even a shrinking future.

The sky was wheeling round as it did against the cone of a turning ship. He drove himself to stand up; a new objective in his head. He would see Barbara Hulse again. Show her what the Lasmec system meant.

He went off at a tangent choosing one of the five palmate roof spreads at random and when he reached the end, cut himself a way in.

It was a food staple store and at ground level there were two fork-lift trucks parked in a bay.

As he swung one out into the exit lane, countermen came running and one stopped off to grab up a video. It had to be a direct run.

The clumsy truck, with its top hamper in a frenetic sway lurched down the high street. Kirby was nearly out on his feet. He could feel blood, sticky, down his left side, vision clouded and cleared.

Behind him, the mob gathered for the kill. They could see that he was far gone as the truck weaved from side to side. When they rounded a bend to find it snagged up against an overhang with its tracks still churning, there was a howl.

But Kirby was not aboard. In a clear spell, he had waited for the turn and jumped as he was masked. When they reached it, he was crossing the canal for the houses of the village.

Maynard himself gave the new line, 'He's hiding out in the old houses. Get a cordon round and search every one.'

Barbara Hulse turned from her window with a sense that

she had lived through the scene in part before. He was standing where she had expected to see him and in the same state of disrepair. But vision and reality carried differing emotional charge.

He was seeing her through a red film which made a subjective colour change, giving her blue, transparent caftan a gamboge tint. He said thickly, 'Rapunzel, Rapunzel let down your hair' and crumpled full length on her parquet.

He did not appreciate that his request was unnecessary, that a cowl of shining silk fell over his head as she knelt beside him and then slowly moved him to her own bed.

When the posse arrived, she had cleaned him up. Broken out a medical pack and run an instant suture along his open wound.

It was Maynard himself at the door and she met him with a book in her hand like a latter-day Lady Macbeth.

Chapter Nine

Maynard said, 'That fool commander has gone over the edge. Turned killer. Has he been here?' He was looking past her into the torchlit room, holding a laser with its catch down.

'It isn't long since he came back in *Europa*. Hadden sent an escort for him and he went off to report what we had found.'

'There was a power failure. He slipped them in the black-out.'

'Perhaps he distrusted Hadden. Why was he sent for?'

Maynard pushed into the room. 'Look, Barbara, there's no time now to go into this. He was a trouble maker. Politically unreliable. Hadden was right to arrest him.'

'So it was an arrest?'

'Yes and made too late. Hadden is dead.'

'Kirby killed him?'

Something in her voice brought Maynard round to a direct confrontation. His voice was coldly deliberate as he said, 'I believe you have a certain sympathy with his ideas. Be careful. Fortunately, he won't live long enough for it to matter. You'll come to the sensible view. You live in the world as it is.'

'In which you are a man of power.'

'In which you have been used to a position of power.'

'You have not asked what we found on the first moon.'

'We can talk about that at tomorrow's council meeting. You can give the report yourself.'

'Commander Kirby should be there.'

'He won't be. He's been declared an outlaw. Make no mistake, he'll be found and killed before morning.'

Barbara Hulse had a moment to wonder what the pyramids would make of it. Justification that they were dealing with a

148

barbaric tribe not long down from the trees. She had no time to stop Maynard as he went casually past her towards the kitchen and swung out of line to dodge through the bedroom door.

Her skin crawled, as though the laser beam was cutting into her own flesh. She hardly heard Maynard as he passed her again on his way out. 'I say again, take care and let me know at once if he comes here. Are you all right?'

'Yes, I'm all right. Just tired. We had a heavy trip.'

Outside, above the glow of the town lights, there was a brighter flare. Noise of a rocket ship in its retro phase.

Maynard said, 'The corvette back. Mowat's cut it very short. Now we'll have him. He'll try to get to the pad.'

At the door, he stopped long enough to deliver an oblique parting shot. 'The Lasmec organization is a long way from here. Make no mistake, Barbara, one way or another you'll honour your contract. Remember that.'

She heard him call to a group outside and then their withdrawing steps on the path.

When she ran into the bedroom, it was empty and she stood stock still in bewilderment looking at a neatly straightened bed.

Kirby, dropping heavily behind her, brought her round with a cry. He steadied himself by putting both hands on her shoulders. For the first time in a human relationship she was totally unsure of herself.

He saw that her eyes were very bright, almost all pupil. Hair falling everywhichway in a pale cascade, taking shifting warm texture from the torchlight. After many years he had reached his Ithaca. After much trafficking with shadows he had found a person who was real for him.

Very slowly, he bent his arms, so that she had to move towards him. Although it needed no answer, he asked, 'Why did you not tell Maynard I was here? You know the penalty for giving comfort to an outlaw?'

She was so close that she had to look up to keep on meeting

149

his eyes. A practised shake of her head and her hair was back in a shining fall.

Physical contact caused no break in the communication building between them. In a curious sense, he could feel his own chest as though from her side of the sensory fence and she could feel his body with her breasts taut and pneumatic against him. Self consciousness was melting out. When his head came down and their lips met, it was only one, indeed the least, of the bonds between them.

When she could speak, she said, 'Grant. I can see, in a way, the mechanism of that pyramid form. It's a kind of love. Dissolving into another identity. I didn't believe it could happen to me.'

'Or me. MC^2 equates with love. Something known for a long time but not understood. Eros makes the whole world tick. I'd reached a stage, just before I got to Hadden, when I didn't care whether I survived or not. Now I do. And it may be too late. *Cossack*'s back.'

'Yes. But you can't do anything about it. You're hurt. Maynard won't come back here. Lie down. I'll get in touch with Mowat.'

'Maynard will be back all right. As soon as he's checked out the houses along here, he'll know that yours was the only one without a thorough search.'

He put his hands on either side of her head underneath her hair, delighting in the fine symmetry of structure, curve of bone, cool silk against his knuckles. 'I want an infinity of time to make love to you.'

'We'll join the pyramid set.'

'I'm not that advanced, I'm glad to say. Just simple one-to-one equations at this stage.'

Her hands were behind his head, fingers laced, pulling it down for an interim dividend.

But professionalism dies hard. Faint and distant as it was, a new star was moving in the gravisphere of Triopus. He saw it over her shoulder through the bedroom window, crossing just above the arc of the second moon which had begun its passage of the night sky. It was, he judged, a rocket ship and it was working its way into an orbit to come down to their planet.

Grant Kirby said, 'Either there will be time for us, or there will not. If there is not, we can't do anything about it. If there is, it will come after we have worked out this situation. Get yourself into something practical and we'll move on.'

'Practical for what?'

'Don't mess about, Barbara, there's another ship coming in. Have a thought for military discipline and put your pants on.'

'Aye, Aye, Sir.'

It was a lighter side of the Lasmec executive, which would once have seemed odd; but in their comfortable unity seemed right and reasonable.

'How's your side?'

'The sutures'll hold up unless I have to do a manual strangulation job on Maynard.'

At the door, she took his arm, 'I don't want to leave, but I know we have to. Gook luck, my darling.' The old words came naturally. Somewhere along the line, she must have read some of the ancient romances.

Outside, they stood flat against their adobe wall and looked away from the town lights across the village. Figures were moving about down the street, hand torches making K's and Y's of light against a dark backdrop.

Cossack was glowing cherry red, not three hundred metres distant. Grey mist dropped in a shroud as Mowat put out a coolant and she disappeared. Movement round the pad suggested that Maynard had put a cordon round. Mowat would have to watch it or he would find a political commissar on his back.

The same thought must have struck *Cossack*'s acting commander. Tague's voice came up on the outside tannoy speaking from the mist like an oracle. 'Keep away from this site. This is military zone.'

A small globule of orange flame cracked down and splayed out from the ground like a water burst. Forward movement checked. There was a single sharp scream from one who had already gone too near.

Kirby said, 'Hadden was on a link-up in his own suite. I'll get back there and talk to Tom.'

'I'll go.'

'Not a chance.'

'Both then.'

Kirby stopped arguing. Since he had lost no more blood, he was feeling better. The puckered ridge of the patent suture was holding up, a tribute to the medical design team which had made up the pack. But he had nothing to spare to insist on a separation, which he did not want anyway. Their time together was likely to be short.

At the town's edge they stopped in penumbra. Then they went on with his arm companionably round her waist, feeling the supple movement of her hip.

Round the jammed fork-lift a group of men still hung about. They had heard the announcement, but wisely considered it was uneconomic to keep a dog and do your own barking. Let the security files get shot up. There was even a certain malicious satisfaction in hoping that some might.

Kirby was less than ten metres off, when a short, dapper man, who was talking with a cigarette moving jerkily in the corner of his mouth, saw him out of the tail of his eye. He stopped in mid gesture, with a gulp that turned the glowing tip onto his cheek and put him out of communication. But his motor reflexes were a credit to the evolutionary tide which had washed him to this far shore. He dived for the fork-lift and disappeared into its cab as though by sleight of hand.

It set a useful tone. Nothing spreads better than panic.

Kirby's image as a maniac-killer got a free boost. One man found himself alone against the far wall, recognized that whichever way he ran he was an easy target, opted for glory and took off towards the searching security force.

Kirby let him go. Maynard was bound to find out within minutes and bring his guards back to town. He said, 'Not far. Do you know which is Hadden's suite?'

'If I say "yes" won't you mind?'

'Why should I? Oh, I see. Well, yes. Yes, I would. I'd prefer it if you'd never spoken to Hadden or anybody else for that matter. On the other hand nothing you ever did is important now.'

'Whatever I did?'

'Only the present has any meaning. The past is a fossil. For us, our future, if we have one, is not bound by our past.' Even as he said it, he wondered how he would react if she had indeed been one of Hadden's visitors.

Whatever she would have answered, was lost in action. A guard, left to patrol the radial appeared like a snap target out of the intersection ahead and left. Kirby in spite of his high-minded chat was the less surprised of the two and caught the man fair and square in his chest as he turned into the street.

Behind them, an unarmed mob was cautiously following up, persuaded that togetherness gave individual guarantee of immortality. They filled the street from edge to edge, silent now and coming to a dead stop when Kirby turned round.

One more block and the admin complex was in sight with movement under the porch and a car waiting on its skids.

Barbara said, 'That's *Philadelphia*'s car. It's the pennant.'

It moved as she spoke, sidling out of cover and coming down towards them. At the same time they were seen by the group on the patio. Three guards ran out hauling a wide angle scatter gun, turning it to spray down the street.

Whoever was piloting the car saw the danger and dropped to a half metre above ground, coming on in a line which masked them from the gunner. When he reached them he slewed to a stop and the entry port sliced back.

Greta Scott, a rich pink with excitement and unusual exertion, said, 'Do be quick. We've been looking for you *everywhere.*'

From the other port, Kirby saw that the gunner was hampered by the crowd at their back. His two aides were signalling for people to clear away. Certainly, fifty civilian dead would take some explaining.

Men were trampling on each other to get from under and the press was thinning. Any second the balance of feasibility would be met.

Scholes at the console said, 'Hold fast,' and lifted them in a straight take off to the car's limit.

In some ways it solved the gunner's problem. There was nothing else to bother about and he swung his barrel with the firing bar down.

For psychological effect, the riot gun had a crimson tracer, and the beam writhed out like a rope of blood. They felt it whip into the undercarriage, then Scholes sideslipped left over a roof and they saw it flicking harmlessly into the night sky.

Scholes said, 'We won't be popular with *Philly*'s captain. He lent us this crate on strict terms that we took it back intact.'

Greta went into explanation, 'We heard the broadcast. Just about. Static's going worse. So Captain Renshaw got on to *Philadelphia* and they lent us the car. We saw *Cossack* come in. But communication's *terrible*. Really I believe there's something big building up. We've been all over looking for you.'

'Where now, Commander?' Scholes was having trouble. The small sonar screen was a mass of bright lines. 'Nothing works any more. There's only direct manual.'

Kirby tried to think, but he felt that he was grappling with a problem in a world of cotton wool. He managed, 'Can we raise *Cossack*?'

'Not a chance.'

154

'They might hear us. Send out a continuous call. Take us up to the main lock.'

Barbara Hulse had been busy at the medekit locker and brought him a non-spill beaker of protein syrup. She put an arm round his shoulders and made him drink. Then she shoved him firmly back in his seat, zipped down his coveralls and held a diagnostic-regulator cup to his chest. Fine hollow needles found their way, sensitively, below the skin. Made their assessment and decanted measured serums.

The warmth of it dissolved the tensions in his head. He could feel it like a heater melting ice in his veins. *Cossack* was towering dead ahead when he knew exactly what there was to do.

Mowat met them at the lock, visor hinged back, clearly glad to have a second opinion.

'Electronics are all to hell, Grant. You'll have seen the ship coming in. Massey thinks it's *Gurkha,* but it's more guesswork. There's a field that blanks everything out. Much more and internal circuits will be shot.'

The wall video crackled into life with Massey's face just recognizable in criss-cross lines of interference. There was urgency in his voice, 'Captain. Something big happening over in the town. Tearing up.'

Direct vision ports were enough to see by. Dawson City was being systematically shredded.

Working on minimum speech levels Kirby went round the crew. 'I want seven volunteers for a one-way ticket. Use Action Station check lights for yes.' Without a flicker every bulb on his crew panel glowed green. The line had taken one step forward and he was still bearing the onus of selection.

Without a break in continuity, he took the hardest decision he had ever made. 'Captain Mowat, take the car. Railton, Scholes, Gilmore, Richardson, Corness, Devon, go with you. Get over to *Europa*, tell them to blast off. Crash action. Parking orbit. *Philadelphia* same drill. Leave Greta and Barbara with *Europa*. Now. Move.

Barbara Hulse was looking at him in open disbelief. 'Grant. You can't. . . .'

But he was already pushing her out along the apron. He would remember her eyes with their look of hurt and betrayal for the rest of his life. But what he had in mind would make that, anyway, a short term chore.

In a count of twenty, he was in his own control room sealing up in the fastest time he had ever recorded, with urgent bleeps sounding through the ship and thrust vibrating the shell as Scaiff cut procedure and went into crash lift-off.

The scanner was a bright blank. In direct vision, he saw a black fissure open in the end block of the distant buildings. Internal ribbing poked out as pressure from the tension-cladding gave way. Two small figures clinging to a length of grille flooring swung free and then fell away into the debris. Then the town's lights went out and *Cossack* began to move.

Kirby spoke to his skeleton crew. He had saved seven for the squadron, if and when it arrived. The rest were prime space-men and their loss was a bitter necessity; but he could not be sure of success with less. 'Hear this. Objective is to destroy the fourth moon. We shall do it. But *Cossack* is the bomb. Lieutenant Scaiff break seals and be ready to escalate the drive for a breakaway reaction. We'll blast out a pit and put *Cossack* in it. There's no other way.'

Every mission was a gamble. They had lived with the possibility from their first days in the service. If it was not now it would be later. If it was not later it would be now. Scaiff said simply, 'Check,' and began to dismantle the elaborate system of safety devices which had been built in to stop him doing just that.

In the last wisps of atmosphere, Tague said, 'Interference is less.' Following on his heels, Massey said, 'Commander, the newcomer is *Gurkha*. I can read her. Have you a message?'

Kirby was already checking the squadron list. Greyson in *Gurkha*. Greyson. Junior to himself on the list. A great man for protocol. Regarded as a political appointee. Well that was all right. He could look after the two freighters. Shepherd them back to the main force if there was nothing left down below to bother about. He said, 'Call *Gurkha*.'

Two minutes and Greyson was head and shoulders on the scanner. A smooth man from what they could see through the oblong panel of a new-type visor. Long oval face with a small fair moustache. Currently looking worried. 'Greyson. What goes on, Commander?'

Kirby reflected that it would be a grade A genius who knew that, but he said, 'Nothing good. Hostiles on one of the moons. They're tearing up the base with a concentrated field. I'm going in now to neutralize. There's not much time.

'You have two freighters coming up and the can in orbit. I'll leave it to you to sort out. My reading is you should rejoin the convoy. Get Martinez to halt on the limits of this gravisphere. Use the ships to ferry people back. It'll take time, but there's nothing for them here.'

Greyson's lines of *angst* deepened.

He said, 'You know they won't do that. What's the setup? The squadron will keep them out of trouble. It can't be so bad.'

Confirmation that it could be, came from his own communications team. They saw him turn his head to look at instrumentation panels. Simultaneously Massey said, 'Holy cow. Look at that transport.'

Sitting plum in its parking orbit, the satellite had given the Triopusians every chance to set it up for the full treatment. Massey had it centred on his screen. Ugly, functional, without grace, it had never been anybody's friend. Now it had a purple bloom like a ripe Autumn fruit. As they watched, it slowly began to redden. It was being eaten up by thermal concentration. Re-entry conditions had unfairly come out to meet it.

Above Sector D lock, a circular chute extruded itself and

for a count of twenty was maintained like a gargoyle feature on a rain gutter. Before it crumpled away, six survival capsules had ejected themselves; shining translucent rain drops, which dispersed as asterisks of white gas in the grilling heat.

Whatever qualities of mind the pyramids might have, it was now certain that the conventional Triopusians were still firmly committed to the violence and destruction of average man.

Kirby snapped, 'Get to it, Commander, there's nothing here, believe me. Even if I succeed in destroying the moon base, the planet itself is a phoney. No better than a mirage. Colonization Ministry will have to think again.'

Even as he said it, he was debating its truth. Reality was a relative thing. If enough people accepted it, might they not create the machinery to maintain it in fact as the pyramids had done? But it would demand greater and more fundamental co-operation than his own race was yet prepared for.

Greyson, saving face, said, 'It would be good sense to hold the convoy at the perimeter. I'll leave it to the executive committee to decide what follows. Do you need help?'

'Keep moving. Watch out for the freighters. When the moon goes you can send one of them down to organize the survivors.' It crossed his mind to add, 'Give my love to Dr Barbara Hulse,' but he edited it out. It was too private for public transmission and there was nothing else he had to send.

'Check.'

The screen blanked as Kirby snapped down the switch and brought in their target which Massey had been holding on a miniature.

They were less than five thousand kilometres away and surface detail was very good. It was in no way different from the moon they had visited. Barren, silver-grey, pock-marked with regular craters.

Top left, a pit larger than any other showed a depth of two thousand metres to a glass-smooth floor like the arena of an amphitheatre. It was ready made as a starting point for further excavation and Kirby said, 'There it is, Navigation One. Into the centre of that and we're half-way home.'

Then the heat beam crossed their course, swung back passing again, oscillated four or five times more with a lessening arc and settled to its frying chore.

Heat shields began to glow and direct thermocouples showed seven-eighths of re-entry maximum. To maintain the course for a full due would bring *Cossack* in as a withered leaf.

Kirby slammed into a major course change and they came round with G pinning them into their couches. In seconds, they were out of the beam and he changed again, cutting its path as the operators swung to follow him.

Nearer, there would be less room to manoeuvre. He was single-minded now, with no thought that his ultimate object was his own death. Change followed change. Tachell blacked. Tague ran the secondary navigation console with his own. Even missing the beam for half the time, cooling gear was coming up to its tolerance threshold.

Moonscape filled the scanner. Now, when the beam struck, heat notched to re-entry plus thirty per cent, as if they had made a long drop through a maximum atmosphere. Ion-flow from the thinning heat shields left a comet tail making a pattern of their flight path.

Kirby saw that his moves were becoming predictable. There was enough pattern in it to help the hidden trackers to anticipate where he would go. Confirmation came when a steep left-hand dive brought him head on into the beam again.

Massey said, hoarsely, labouring to breathe, 'Computerized, by God. Interpolated. Predictable as a dog in a colonnade. We'll never make it now.'

There was bitterness in it. Obliquely telling Kirby that their sacrifice, only marginally useful at best, was a pointless exercise.

He had already seen the light. From a great distance he could sense a new element in his own thinking. A power which he recognized as infinitely subtle and complex was trying to take over. He surrendered his will to it, and was an observer, as a new commander took over *Cossack*.

For the crew, it was the most fantastic fifteen minutes they had ever spent. It seemed that Kirby was taking the ship to the hairsbreadth limit in every direction of its capability and to the physiological barriers of their own endurance. But every time, before the structure failed or a man broke, there was a momentary easing that kept them in business.

Cossack pulled back in full retro, sideslipped, fell away, corkscrewed on a zany trajectory that followed no equation that could be understood. She was thrown about like a random fly with *delirium tremens*. And all the time she was working close to her objective, until Kirby could set her down in a straight run, glowing red, but with every heat shield intact.

As they passed the crater lip, the beam cut out, screened by a half kilometre of dense igneous rock. *Cossack*'s last planet-fall was precise, perfect, at a speed that took her within millimetres of the full compression of her hydraulic jacks. She was still poised digestively before recoil when grey clouds of coolant were billowing out and Kirby was detailing the landing party for its excavation chore.

Every ship in the squadron carried the means to disperse meteoritic lumps which could wander into the trade lanes and wreck a careless navigator. It was part of the work of every deep space patrol. Useless against a minor planet the size of the first moon, it was good enough to carve out a deep grave for the towering ship.

A massive vibrator opened up long shot holes in the smooth rock and Kirby shifted blocks that would have had Cheops twisting his kilt in jealous shame.

When it was finished, a long trench ran from one tripod foot to the centre of the arena. The ship stood like an offset gnomon with its shadow on a sundial disk. The last charge went under the foot to undercut and drop *Cossack* into her burial pit.

Sibley said, 'It's like asking a condemned man to dig his own grave and shooting him so that he falls in.'

'You should worry. We won't be far behind.' Now that the work was done, there was time to think and Parkes was not enthusiastic about what he saw.

Working like a maniac-wrecker, Scaiff had stripped out every safety device in the power pack. *Cossack* was converted into an immense nuclear bomb. The reactor was already over its threshold and escalating on a one-way ticket, when Kirby blew the last charge from a screen of massive blocks a hundred metres from the trench.

There were seven of them to see their ship go and they stood in line to watch.

Tague, as acting captain, rose to the occasion with a clumsy salute. Tachell, his second in navigation, stood to attention. Scaiff, as architect of the destruction to come, stood with his hands on his hips, a bulbous gnome. Massey, away from his computers, managed to look bewildered even through the impersonal blanket of his gear. Parkes leaned on a rock and looked as though he would have whittled a stick if there had been one handy. Sibley methodically began to reel back the severed line.

Cossack seemed to hesitate as though she could not believe that this was happening to her. Then she began to turn on her two standing feet with the shattered leg crumpling away. Momentum gathered, but in the low gravity she seemed to fall like a long balloon, soundless, a dream sequence.

When she was there, although already carrying the burgeoning seeds of death, she was a familiar landmark and some solution had seemed possible. When she had gone there was a finality about it which thrust home.

Kirby thought, 'What am I doing here? I could have kept Barbara on *Cossack* and got to hell out of this. Left the colony to take care of itself. I'd done all that was humanly possible to warn them.' But it was not that simple. He knew that he had not done it for the colonists in the last analysis but for himself. 'Whoever knows to do good and does not do it—to that man that is sin.' There was no evading responsibility to one's own truth.

There was still work to do and it would fill the minutes before the moon went up. Keep their minds off it. He said, 'Well done, all. A very neat and workmanlike mission. We'll take the rest of these charges and shift some rocks back into that hole. Dust to dust. Ashes to ashes.'

Cossack lay in the depths like a shattered column.

Chapter Ten

Europa was beating up to the rag-bag of debris which had been the transport before Barbara Hulse came out of her zombie trance and began asking questions.

On the strength of her mathematical reputation she had been sited in the command cabin as a general dogsbody on the communications net. So far her contribution had been nil and Greta had stopped pushing data her way. There was, anyway, not much pressure on. Interference was less than it had been at any time since their arrival and the computers had settled for an honest-Hack service.

Renshaw brought them smoothly up, to pace beside the ruins with a probe out to seek for any biological flotsam.

On the main scanner, they could see *Cossack* ducking and weaving as she worked ever closer to the fourth moon. When she disappeared into a crater mouth, Barbara snapped into life. Ignoring procedures, she used the communications priority board to speak direct to Mowat who was chief guest on the command island and filling the co-pilot slot. 'Captain Mowat. What has *Cossack* gone to do?'

Mowat automatically checked round before answering. Found that they could spare a minute for a clarifying chat and said, 'There's only one way to destroy an asteroid that size. He'll bury the ship and let the plant escalate.'

'But they'll all be killed!'

'That's why we're here. There wasn't much time, but every man volunteered and Commander Kirby made his choice.'

'He didn't give me any choice.'

Mowat was in a brand new role as a comforter and looked round for any shifting dial to give him an excuse for breaking clear. But *Europa* was rock steady and no new instructions were coming up from *Gurkha*. He managed, 'He couldn't take you. How could he condemn you to death? How could he have a clear mind knowing what he was going to do to you? You saw how difficult it was to get there. That was a superb, single-minded bit of navigation.'

She was not a Lasmec for nothing. Without answering she switched through to Renshaw. 'Captain Renshaw, this is a civilian ship.'

It was a statement of fact and his 'Check' came as no surprise.

'It is chartered by the Ministry of Colonization and under direction of the Executive Committee.'

'That is so, Dr Hulse.'

'As the only member of the executive here present, you are responsible to me.'

'Technically, yes. But I remind you that, in space, a captain directs his ship and in any matter concerning the professional work of the ship, he has the last word. You know the articles.'

'But here we are not technically in space. There is no time to go on with the argument. I direct you to follow *Cossack* on to that moon and bring off her crew.'

There was silence on the net. Renshaw thought it served him right for putting a civilian where she could still speak. He said, 'You saw that they only just got there. *Europa* is no corvette. It would be no help to Commander Kirby to sacrifice this ship.'

'I know that. But the interference is less. Perhaps there will be less opposition. We could try.'

'It will have to be cleared with the new Commander. He is in authority over all craft in this gravisphere.'

Tom Mowat saw the danger. Greyson was likely to take the negative line and underwrite Kirby's own command decision. He came in quickly with, 'There's no time for that. I agree with Dr Hulse. We should try. Conditions have altered. If we can't make it, then we have to pull out.'

It was tough on Renshaw, but the last gloss was a let out. They could see how it worked. He began to call the shots to put *Europa* on course.

Problems were already multiplying round Greyson. Unable to reach *Cossack*, the Triopusians had made the judgement that the only other threat could come from the new corvette and swung their heat beam her way. *Gurkha* began to twist and dive as though a mania had her captain in its grip. Unsupported by local industry, he was no match for the tracking gear of the fourth moon. Gauges levelled at re-entry plus twenty per cent. *Gurkha* began to fry.

This ill wind stuck to traditional form for *Europa*. Coming in at a low angle, her only problem was navigation. With a less favourable power-to-weight ratio than a corvette, she could not afford the same last minute decisions on course data. But there was no overheating. That angle was absorbed by *Gurkha* as though there had been a deliberate decoy plan set up between them.

At the last, Renshaw called for corrective retro with the crater rim less than ten kilometres below him and *Europa* lobbed in like a ball into a bunker.

For Kirby, it was a moment of ambivalent loading. With the interment done he had brought his party back to an overhang of the crater wall. They could have climbed out, but once *Cossack* went over the edge, there would be nothing to choose between any part of the moon's surface.

Silent they had to be, in a no-atmosphere setup. Only a deliberate seeking of a *confidente* on a one-to-one link would be effective in the roar of static on the radio bands. Nobody made that choice. They leaned, backs against the rock, waiting for eternity to blossom from *Cossack's* grave.

Grant Kirby was filling time trying to evaluate consciousness as a fact of life. Sensitive, by his sense of loss, soberly melancholy, not wanting to be dissipated as impersonal energy for cosmic rebuilding elsewhere, he was challenging the view that consciousness was the sum of all the information that his computer mind had put in store.

If that was all, it didn't make much sense. Even the present ploy was inescapable on that count. Just a conditioned reflex, predictable when you knew what was in the box? Not entirely that. Had he done it to get Barbara out of it with a chance to live?

At this moment in time, he had to be honest. Waiting for his leap into the dark, there was no room for any self-deceit. Down at rock bottom that was not it. It was for himself that he had done it. He had seen that it was a possible action, that in the circumstances it ought to be done. One more victim of the sense of ought, which made him man and different from any cybernetic device whatever. Having seen it, he could not avoid it. Not doing it would have been something he could not have lived comfortably with, Barbara notwithstanding.

The conclusion brought a kind of peace. He relaxed. Leaned back against the rock. Closed his eyes and saw Barbara Hulse as a brilliant eidetic image. It was a pleasure untinged by any envy or regret. He was glad for the communication there had been between them. They had been lucky. For the majority of people it did not happen at all.

Tague's gauntlet thumping his arm brought him back to the present and *Europa* had a full audience to see her flame briefly down, wobble self-consciously to a dodgy planetfall, and stand flexing on her jacks at the edge of the rough trench.

Grey coolant billowed out and screened her as they ran forward. Two hundred metres of flat skating rink lightly dusted with grit. Fifty metres out from the crater wall and Tague, lumbering along beside Kirby, pitched forward and fell on his face.

Sibley on his far side stopped with Kirby and they had an arm each to lift him, when they saw the back of his suit. Smack between the shoulder blades there was a palm-sized, round hole that might have been made by a meteorite.

Simultaneously, they reached the same answer. Sibley, as the gunner, was a fraction quicker looking back for the point of origin.

Scrambling down the ridge, twenty or more tiny figures in black box-section pressure gear, unlike anything anyone had seen. A small knot of operators manhandling a piece of artillery, standing aside for a second shot. Puff of dust marking a recoil.

Clearly it was a survival from another age. Unable to bring sophisticated weaponry to bear they had dug this one out of store. With that level of accuracy it would be enough.

Kirby thought, 'So long as they don't think about shooting up the ship.' Then he was signalling for flat down and dropping himself like a log. If it had been *Cossack* there, they could have turned the main armament on that cliff and reduced it to rubble, but the freighter had only a few hand lasers, short range.

They were up and running again, passing a gouged-out hole where the second shot had dug in after passing where Sibley's back had been.

He felt an itch between his shoulder blades. This was much worse than waiting for *Cossack* to go up.

Farther left, Art Scaiff missed the rhythm and stayed down. Less than fifty metres to go and the freight elevator was coming down in the thinning gas with Corness and Devon swinging a tripod-mounted heavy laser. It was not much, but it would reach the rim with its dissuasive needle beam.

Parkes bought it as they reached the shadow of the tripod and then Corness had the range and was pricking fatal holes in the space gear of the Triopusian gunners. He cleared an area fifty metres every way round the gun as a crowded elevator tray took them up into the freight lock.

As soon as the inner shield sliced back, Kirby was on to the command cabin from an intercom.

Renshaw had used time to rig emergency couches in the

freight bay and Kirby stayed out of his straps long enough to say on the general net, 'Crash action. Lift her off. Thank you.'

Barbara Hulse, hearing his voice against all expectation, felt her heart hammering in the hollow confines of her private shell and the cardio gauge on her console went into a small flurry which had nothing to do with failure in any life-support system. She was also unreasonably piqued that he had not spoken directly to her.

Work is the best therapy. Greta shoved a mass of data her way and she was instantly committed in the exacting math of finding *Europa*'s new handling characteristics with four extra bodies badly placed in the tail.

Renshaw was not immediately concerned. He knew that he had to get her up in the shortest possible space of time and was prepared to go into debate about where they were going when it was sure that it was a meaningful question.

In the main scanner, they saw more figures pressing over the rim of the crater. The field piece had a new team. They saw the puff of dust that spelled out a shot fired as *Europa* began to move.

It was her most vulnerable time. Without enough thrust to stabilize her, she was susceptible to any lateral force.

When it came it was as though *Europa* had been kicked in the tail by a rogue dinosaur. Collision alarms set up a frenetic clang on every companion. The ship absorbed the energy of the blow in a turning movement round her centre and the cone began to dip. Then the thrust started to bite. She was charging back in a bid to run herself up the barrel of the gun.

If they had stuck to it, the gunners could not have missed. But the sight of the huge ship with its elongating fire ball bearing down on them was too much. They broke and scrambled clear.

Renshaw was banging his console with both fists, shouting, 'Lift it. Lift it, you crazy bitch. Get your head up.'

They were skimming the crest with pumice dust flaring back in a grey cloud shot with orange flame.

Barbara Hulse had a direct vision port above her head and was spitting distance from a man lying on his back on the rock face. A Triopusian, but different from those of the first expedition's film record. A savage face. Terrified now. Lips moving soundlessly inside his visor as the great cylinder bored close overhead to sear open his fragile shell and fill his shouting mouth with pumice dust.

Europa began to climb, clawing her way for space.

Travelling blind in the freight bay, Kirby was doing a private count down. He had reached, much to his own surprise, a hundred and seventeen when *Cossack* made her last military contribution.

Blown like a leaf in a typhoon *Europa* picked up unscheduled acceleration which ripped improvised couches free and turned the loading bay into smash.

Mowat, in his last split second of consciousness, shoved the stick on auto. Then *Europa* was working it out alone, using the forethought her designers had built in.

In her favour, all electronic interference stopped. Computers had a clear run at the physical facts as far as they were measurable.

For a full minute, elemental chaos was come again. A thin thread of order-making reason probed into the cloud. The minds on the first moon looked in and watched the ship salvage its sleeping load.

Grant Kirby surfaced from an infinite depth of dark blue water, broke through its shining corrugated roof into the bright light of the freight bay. He knew at once from the feel of the ship that she was stabilized in orbital flight. Remembering the number one one seven, he ravelled back the associative chain and stabbed at his release clips.

His acceleration couch was wedged across the inner hatch as a retaining wall for all the gear that had broken free. When he pulled it clear, there was a general drift of material to the notional deck. That meant the gravity simulator was on at about point-three.

He plugged himself into the intercom and got no signal, so cranked back the hatch on its ratchet and pinion manual shift. It took him two minutes in mounting impatience then he climbed through and went quickly along the companion to the control room hatch.

Missing out on mural interest, it was nevertheless like breaking into the burial chamber of a royal tomb. Still figures on every couch. Screens blank. Auto pilot playing it cool on a settled course.

There was nothing to do but wait. He picked his way through the bodies to the communication centre. Greta Scott, eyes closed, face pale and set. Then Barbara. He snapped back her harness, eased out neck seals and tipped back her visor. Her long hair which had been piled hurriedly on top of her head fell in a warm aromatic stream over his hands.

Fingers on either side of her head marvelling at the familiar feel and shape of it as though it had been part of the furniture of his mind for all his life. He kissed her forehead very gently.

Barbara Hulse surfaced into the world of sense and had some difficulty in sorting out the first sensory stimuli preferred for analysis. But she knew at a very deep level that the hands holding her were friendly. A long training in higher mathematics sharpens the mind. She said with quick classification, 'Grant,' and followed up with a question to show that the scientific spirit never sleeps, 'Are you all right?'

'I am now.'

There would be time for their personal showdown. They both recognized it and filed it away as an inevitable future confrontation. There was no avoidance of it when she changed the subject, 'What happened to the fourth moon?'

He helped her out of her couch. Mowat was looking round and Renshaw was lifting his head. Another minute and *Europa*

170

would be ready to direct her own future. They started a roving search of the gravisphere.

Philadelphia came up, a motionless silver fish on a black marble slab. The first moon. Second and third moons, differently placed now. Making a huge equilateral triangle with the first and certainly nearer the surface of Triopus.

Of *Gurkha* there was no sign. Nor was there anything to be seen of *New World*. The fourth moon was dwindling away. Still roughly cohesive as an exploded sphere; fissured and fragmented so that it was a collection of meteoritic trash travelling in company. Its new-found urge would take it out of the gravisphere to an ultimate RV in a distant part of the galaxy. Old bricks for new building.

Renshaw had a team. He put them to work bringing *Europa* to cruise fifty metres from her sister ship. Some human solidarity on an emptying set.

In radio conditions clearer than at any time yet Greta Scott tried to raise Dawson City.

On the main scanner, the ground base came up as an entity still. Outlying building blocks were torn and twisted as though by a hurricane but the centre appeared intact. There was a curious violet bloom on its metallic skin, but otherwise there was no damage.

Grant Kirby wedged in between Renshaw and Mowat on the command island said, 'What's the state of the ship, Captain? Can you put us down?'

'Not a chance. The last shot bitched up a jack. It's a major repair job. Without docking facilities it's a repair we can't make. I'll have to stay parked until the main force check in. Or go home.'

'Hang on then. I'll go down in *Philadelphia*.'

It was dawn on Triopus when the ship settled for a precise, copybook planetfall on her familiar pad. Streaks of pale viridian and cadmium yellow made a backdrop for the dark twisted girderwork of the wrecked city.

As soon as the freight elevator touched down at ground level, they could sense a change in the atmosphere of the place.

With a feeling for protocol, as the representatives of Earth planet making a gesture, they were dressed with some care. Barbara Hulse in brilliant, powder-blue metalcloth. Greta in crimson; Kirby, Mowat, Railton and Scholes in the white uniforms of the military space service.

Philadelphia's half-track freight trolley took them off the pad and met waist-deep vegetation like elephant grass.

'That's it. That's the difference. Just look at the trees—' Greta Scott's voice was half an octave over normal pitch.

She had a point. Overnight the vegetable life had suffered a sea change. It was lush to tropical levels. Trees on the perimeter were towering sequoias, bushes were trebled, luxuriant, heavily aromatic.

They churned through to a towpath, followed the canal and cut in again towards the reception area.

Evidence of the heat blast came as the caterpillar tracks bit into the first stretch of metalled roadway. They were leaving furrows as the surface crumbled away. Even the slight vibration of the light trolley was enough to disturb the balance and building blocks on either side began to settle.

Kirby had time to spin the trolley in its own length and slam back at full thrust.

When he stopped, they saw the disintegration spreading back. Slowly and silently like the dissolving of a mirage, the remaining buildings crumbled away.

In a count of ten there was only a dust pall. As they watched, the cleared area reformed, bushes and trees established themselves. Except for its new look of opulence, their corner of Triopus was regenerated as it had been.

'Somebody's there'—Mowat had a heavy duty laser on the forward hoop of the trolley and then stood stupidly looking

172

at two figures separating out from the regenerate foreground and walking towards them.

Kirby said, 'You won't need that, Tom' and went forward to meet them.

They were Triopusians. Tabal and Comana walking unhurriedly as though they had been out for a morning stroll from their village.

Hands in the universal human mime for greeting, Comana said, 'You have done what we could have done, but there was always a latent scruple about turning against our own kind. Too late to save your people though.'

There was a rebuke in it. Mild enough, but Kirby felt the injustice of it. 'You have been too long above the battle. There has to be conflict.'

Barbara had followed him, a shining figure in the strengthening light of a sun balancing like a penny on the rim of a plate. She said, 'Where do we stand now? What is your attitude towards us?'

Tabal was looking at her in simple appreciation, as though she filled an aesthetic dimension which even the permutations of the complex minds had not hit. 'If all the visitors from Earth planet had been as you are, we might have reached a different conclusion.'

Mathematician coming through strongly in the morning light, she ignored the compliment and pressed for an answer. 'What is your conclusion?'

'Without undervaluing you, I say again that you could not understand us. That is a simple truth. Sometime in the future your people may be ready to come here. But not now. Not yet. You must go back to your own planet.'

'That is all very well,' Kirby was speaking to Comana, 'but there is a fleet of transports on the way. Many people. They cannot be turned back. Do you intend to harm them?'

'We do not harm anyone. Action has already been taken. They will not arrive.'

173

'What have you done?'

'They have been diverted. There are ample supplies, equipment which will support life for many generations. They will go on travelling in space, but they will not arrive here.'

'And that is not harming them?' Barbara's voice had a bitter edge.

'It is all a matter of organizing themselves. A good life is possible anywhere. What did they intend to do here that they cannot do in their travelling cities? They were preparing to cover themselves in like moles.'

It was a line of argument which had already risen in Kirby's own mind and he felt that the ground had been unfairly taken from under his feet.

There was nothing to do then except take the ships back. Report to the Colonization Ministry. Stop any second wave of immigrants. That would take some doing and he did not fancy the job. Radio probes might find the wandering colony. Ships might be sent to ferry the people back. A long and costly fiasco. Boris Martinez would have something to stroke his forehead about.

He asked, 'What will you do? Will you live in the villages again?'

Tabal said, 'You have altered the set of the moons. As you see, there has been a change in the vegetation. It would not be easy to change back to the conditions we prefer. Not now. Perhaps not at all. There is plenty of time for that.'

Certainly they had all the time in the world and did not intend to use any of it in circular argument. When Barbara began another question, she was talking to empty air.

Below the towering bulk of *Philadelphia*, they waited in silence for the elevator to come down. Each one busy with his own thoughts.

Grant Kirby was coming to a decision which he recognized had been made already in the hinterland of his mind for some

174

time. Bringing it into consciousness seemed no more than recognition of an established fact.

He was standing with Barbara outside the group and when he spoke to her, he knew what her reaction would be. Harmony with another discrete human being which he had never expected to find. There had been enough of movement between stars like a galactic hobo. This place of clear light and quietness was his anchorage in the eye of the wind.

He said, 'I shall not go back.'

'I was hoping you would say that. Where shall we live?'

'We?'—it was pure rhetoric. The equation was satisfied. Speech was not necessary between them.

'You forget. I am the only remaining member of the civil branch. There can't be a military arm without a supporting public.'

But no decision is entirely straightforward, there were details to finalize with Mowat, depositions to be made. When it was done and they were standing alone away from the pad, the sun was nudging up to its meridian.

Flame blossomed below the ship and she began to lift. Slowly, and then with gathering urge, she took the first step of her fantastic journey. Arrow slim, with a perfection of functional form, she was a testament to the progress of their race which gave them both a certain pride.

They saw her pace alongside *Europa* and both ships wheeled to pick up a course for Earth planet.

Mowat had insisted on leaving the half-track trolley loaded with stores, but they left it and walked hand in hand beside the canal.

Barbara broke away and ran ahead to stand before a piece of organic engineering which had certainly not been there before. She called out, 'Grant, look at this! The pyramids don't mind us being here. Look what they've given us.'

Fruit hung heavily on the branches. There was no cosmic

mystery about it. It had once been a very common feature of Earth's husbandry and they both knew it well from pictures and childhood stories. Something stirred sluggishly amongst the leaves and she flung herself back into his arms.

A serpent head peered out and a long, green and yellow snake writhed its length out of the foliage.

'Grant. It's a joke. They have a sense of humour.'

She twisted free and made deft work of a number of hidden fastenings. Her shining metalcloth suit fell away and she ran forward like a dancer.

When she turned to him again with her hair falling over bare shoulders, an elastic bell of pale electrum, she was holding an apple in each outstretched hand.

Grant Kirby said, 'It figures. Without the fourth moon there is no evil principle on this planet. Without evil how shall we ever congratulate ourselves on being virtuous? Pick some more and give one to that poor dumb beast.'

But her wrists were crossed behind his head and she was hanging like a warm albatross.

Metaphysics would have to choose another day. When the apples dropped to the ground behind him, he edited a gloss about Newton and picked her up.

'You won't hurt your side?'

'On this day of gestures, it can take its chance.'

Over his shoulder, she saw that the tree had gone. But it did not matter. It was a portent. They could stay. They had a future. More particularly, a present.